THE KNIGHT
OF THE SWORDS

CORUM BOOK I

MICHAEL MOORCOCK

THE KNIGHT
OF THE SWORDS

CORUM BOOK 1

TITAN BOOKS

The Knight of the Swords
Print edition ISBN: 9781783291656
E-book edition ISBN: 9781783291649

Published by Titan Books
A division of Titan Publishing Group Ltd
144 Southwark Street, London SE1 0UP

First Titan edition: May 2015
12345678910

Edited by John Davey

A CIP catalogue record for this title is available from the British Library.

Printed and bound in the United States

This book is for Wendy Fletcher

# INTRODUCTION

I N THOSE DAYS there were oceans of light and cities in the skies and wild flying beasts of bronze. There were herds of crimson cattle that roared and were taller than castles. There were shrill, viridian things that haunted bleak rivers. It was a time of gods, manifesting themselves upon our world in all her aspects; a time of giants who walked on water; of mindless sprites and misshapen creatures who could be summoned by an ill-considered thought but driven away only on pain of some fearful sacrifice; of magics, phantasms, unstable nature, impossible events, insane paradoxes, dreams come true, dreams gone awry, of nightmares assuming reality.

It was a rich time and a dark time. The time of the Sword Rulers. The time when the Vadhagh and the Nhadragh, age-old enemies, were dying. The time when Man, the slave of fear, was emerging, unaware that much of the terror he experienced was the result of nothing else but the fact that he, himself, had come into existence. It was one of many ironies connected with Man

MICHAEL MOORCOCK

(who, in those days, called his race "Mabden").

The Mabden lived brief lives and bred prodigiously. Within a few centuries they rose to dominate the westerly continent on which they had evolved. Superstition stopped them from sending many of their ships towards Vadhagh and Nhadragh lands for another century or two, but gradually they gained courage when no resistance was offered. They began to feel jealous of the older races; they began to feel malicious.

The Vadhagh and the Nhadragh were not aware of this. They had dwelt a million or more years upon the planet which now, at last, seemed at rest. They knew of the Mabden but considered them not greatly different from other beasts. Though continuing to indulge their traditional hatreds of one another, the Vadhagh and the Nhadragh spent their long hours in considering abstractions, in the creation of works of art and the like. Rational, sophisticated, at one with themselves, these older races were unable to believe in the changes that had come. Thus, as it almost always is, they ignored the signs.

There was no exchange of knowledge between the two ancient enemies, even though they had fought their last battle many centuries before.

The Vadhagh lived in family groups occupying isolated castles scattered across a continent called by them Bro-an-Vadhagh. There was scarcely any communication between these families, for the Vadhagh had long since lost the impulse to travel. The Nhadragh lived in their cities built on the islands in the seas to the north-west of Bro-an-Vadhagh. They, also, had little contact, even with their closest kin. Both races reckoned themselves invulnerable. Both were wrong.

Upstart Man was beginning to breed and spread like a pestilence across the world. This pestilence struck down the Old

Races wherever it touched them. And it was not only death that Man brought, but terror, too. Willfully, he made of the older world nothing but ruins and bones. Unwittingly, he brought psychic and supernatural disruption of a magnitude which even the Great Old Gods failed to comprehend.

And the Great Old Gods began to know Fear.

And Man, slave of fear, arrogant in his ignorance, continued his stumbling progress. He was blind to the huge disruptions aroused by his apparently petty ambitions. As well, Man was deficient in sensitivity, had no awareness of the multitude of dimensions that filled the universe, each plane intersecting with several others. Not so the Vadhagh or the Nhadragh, who had known what it was to move at will between the dimensions they termed the Five Planes. They had glimpsed and understood the nature of the many planes, other than the five, through which the Earth moved.

Therefore it seemed a dreadful injustice that these wise races should perish at the hands of creatures who were still little more than animals. It was as if vultures feasted on and squabbled over the paralyzed body of the youthful poet who could only stare at them with puzzled eyes as they slowly robbed him of an exquisite existence they would never appreciate, never know they were taking.

"If they valued what they stole, if they knew what they were destroying," says the old Vadhagh in the story, *Now The Clouds Have Meaning*, "then I would be consoled."

It was unjust.

By creating Man, the universe had betrayed the Old Races.

But it was a perpetual and familiar injustice. The sentient may perceive and love the universe, but the universe cannot perceive and love the sentient. The universe sees no distinction between the multitude of creatures and elements which comprise it. All are equal. None is favoured. The universe, equipped with nothing but the materials and the power of creation, continues to create: something of this, something of that. It cannot control what it creates and it cannot, it seems, be controlled by its creations (though a few might deceive themselves otherwise). Those who curse the workings of the universe curse that which is deaf. Those who strike out at those workings fight that which is inviolate. Those who shake their fists, shake their fists at blind stars.

But this does not mean that there are some who will not try to do battle with and destroy the invulnerable.

There will always be such beings, sometimes beings of great wisdom, who cannot bear to believe in an insouciant universe.

Prince Corum Jhaelen Irsei was one of these. Perhaps the last of the Vadhagh race, he was sometimes known as the Prince in the Scarlet Robe.

This chronicle concerns him.

— *The Book of Corum*

BOOK ONE

IN WHICH PRINCE CORUM LEARNS
A LESSON AND LOSES A LIMB

AT CASTLE ERORN

A T Castle Erorn dwelt the family of the Vadhagh prince, Khlonskey. This family had occupied the castle for many centuries. It loved, exceedingly, the moody sea that washed Erorn's northern walls and the pleasant forest that crept close to her southern flank.

Castle Erorn was so ancient that she seemed to have fused entirely with the rock of the huge eminence that overlooked the sea. Outside, it was a splendour of time-worn turrets and salt-smoothed stones. Within, it had moving walls which changed shape in tune with the elements and changed colour when the wind changed course. And there were rooms full of arrangements of crystals and fountains, playing exquisitely complicated fugues composed by members of the family, some living, some dead. And there were galleries filled with paintings brushed on marble and glass by Prince Khlonskey's artist ancestors. And there were libraries filled with manuscripts written by members of both the Vadhagh and the Nhadragh races. And elsewhere in Castle Erorn were rooms of statues, and there were aviaries and menageries, observatories, laboratories, nurseries, gardens, chambers of meditation, surgeries, gymnasia, collections of martial paraphernalia, kitchens, planetaria, museums, conjuratoria, as well as rooms set aside for less specific purposes, or rooms forming the apartments of those who lived in the castle.

Twelve people lived in the castle now, though once five hundred had occupied it. The twelve were Prince Khlonskey, himself, a very ancient being; his wife Colatalarna, who was, in appearance, much younger than her husband; Ilastru and Pholhinra, his twin daughters; Prince Rhanan, his brother; Sertreda, his niece; Corum, his son. The remaining five were retainers, distant cousins of the prince. All had characteristic Vadhagh features: narrow, long skulls; ears that were almost without lobes and tapered flat alongside the head; fine hair that a breeze would make rise like flimsy clouds about their faces; large almond eyes that had yellow centres and purple surrounds; wide, full-lipped mouths and skin that was a strange, gold-flecked rose-pink. Their bodies were slim and tall and well proportioned and they moved with a leisurely grace that made the human gait seem like the shambling of a crippled ape.

Occupying themselves chiefly with remote, intellectual pastimes, the family of Prince Khlonskey had had no contact with other Vadhagh folk for two hundred years and had not seen a Nhadragh for three hundred. No news of the outside world had come to them for over a century. Only once had they seen a Mabden, when a specimen had been brought to Castle Erorn by Prince Opash, a naturalist and first cousin to Prince

Khlonskey. The Mabden—a female—had been placed in the menageries where it was cared for well, but it lived little more than fifty years and when it died was never replaced. Since then, of course, the Mabden had multiplied and were, it appeared, even now inhabiting large areas of Bro-an-Vadhagh. There were even rumours that some Vadhagh castles had been infested with Mabden who had overwhelmed the inhabitants and eventually destroyed their homes altogether. Prince Khlonskey found this hard to believe. Besides, the speculation was of little interest to him or his family. There were so many other things to discuss, so many more complex sources of speculation, pleasanter topics of a hundred kinds.

Prince Khlonskey's skin was almost milk-white and so thin that all the veins and muscles were clearly displayed beneath. He had lived for over a thousand years and only recently had age begun to enfeeble him. When his weakness became unbearable, when his eyes began to dim, he would end his life in the manner of the Vadhagh, by going to the Chamber of Vapours and laying himself on the silk quilts and cushions and inhaling the various sweet-smelling gases until he died. His hair had turned a golden brown with age and the colour of his eyes had mellowed to a kind of reddish purple with pupils of dark orange. His robes were now rather too large for his body, but, although he carried a staff of plaited platinum in which ruby metal had been woven, his bearing was still proud and his back was not bent.

One day he sought his son, Prince Corum, in a chamber where music was formed by the arranging of hollow tubes, vibrating wires and shifting stones. The very simple, quiet music was almost drowned by the sound of Khlonskey's feet on the tapestries, the tap of his staff and the rustle of the breath in his thin throat.

Prince Corum withdrew his attention from the music and gave his father a look of polite enquiry.

"Father?"

"Corum. Forgive the interruption."

"Of course. Besides, I was not satisfied with the work." Corum rose from his cushions and drew his scarlet robe about him.

"It occurs to me, Corum, that I will soon visit the Chamber of Vapours," said Prince Khlonskey, "and, in reaching this decision, I had it in mind to indulge a whim of mine. However, I will need your help."

Now Prince Corum loved his father and respected his decision, so he said gravely, "That help is yours, Father. What can I do?"

"I would know something of the fate of my kinsmen. Of Prince Opash, who dwells at Castle Sarn in the east. Of Princess Lorim, who is at Castle Crachah in the south. And of Prince Faguin of Castle Gal in the north."

Prince Corum frowned. "Very well, Father, if…"

"I know, son, what you think—that I could discover what I wish to know by occult means. Yet this is not so. For some reason it is difficult to achieve intercourse with the other planes. Even my perception of them is dimmer than it should be, try as I might to enter them with my senses. And to enter them physically is almost impossible. Perhaps it is my age…"

"No, Father," said Prince Corum, "for I, too, have found it difficult. Once it was easy to move through the Five Planes at will. With a little more effort the Ten Planes could be contacted, though, as you know, few could visit them physically. Now I am unable to do more than see and occasionally hear those other four planes which, with ours, form the spectrum through which our planet directly passes in its astral cycle. I do not understand why this loss of sensibility has come about."

"And neither do I," agreed his father. "But I feel that it must be portentous. It indicates some major change in the nature of our Earth. This is the chief reason why I would discover something of my relatives and, perhaps, learn if they know why our senses become bound to a single plane. It is unnatural. It is crippling to us. Are we to become like the beasts of this plane, which are aware only of one dimension and have no understanding that the others exist at all? Is some process of devolution at work? Shall our children know nothing of our experiences and slowly return to the state of those aquatic mammals from which our race sprang? I will admit to you, my son, that there are traces of fear in my mind."

Prince Corum did not attempt to reassure his father. "I read once of the Blandhagna," he said thoughtfully. "They were a race based on the Third Plane. A people of great sophistication. But something took hold of their genes and of their brains and, within five generations, they had reverted to a species of flying reptile still equipped with a vestige of their former intelligence— enough to make them mad and, ultimately, destroy themselves completely. What is it, I wonder, that produces these reversions?"

"Only the Sword Rulers know," his father said.

Corum smiled. "And the Sword Rulers do not exist. I understand your concern, Father. You would have me visit these kinsmen of yours and bring them our greetings. I should discover if they fare well and if they have noticed what we have noticed at our Castle Erorn."

His father nodded. "If our perception dims to the level of a Mabden, then there is little point in continuing our race. Find out, too, if you can, how the Nhadragh fare—if this dullness of the senses comes to them."

"Our races are of more or less equal age," Corum murmured. "Perhaps they are similarly afflicted. But did not your kinsman Shulag have something to say, when he visited you some centuries back?"

"Aye. Shulag had it that the Mabden had come in ships from the West and subjugated the Nhadragh, killing most and making slaves of those remaining. Yet I find it hard to believe that the Mabden half-beasts, no matter how great their numbers, would have the wit to defeat Nhadragh cunning."

Prince Corum pursed his lips reflectively. "Possibly they grew complacent," he said.

His father turned to leave the chamber, his staff of ruby and platinum tapping softly on the richly embroidered cloth covering the flagstones, his delicate hand clutching it more tightly than usual. "Complacency is one thing," he said, "and fear of an impossible doom is another. Both, of course, are ultimately destructive. We need speculate no more, for on your return you may bring us answers to these questions. Answers that we can understand. When would you leave?"

"I have it in mind to complete my symphony," Prince Corum said. "That will take another day or so. I will leave on the morning after I finish it."

Prince Khlonskey nodded his old head in satisfaction. "Thank you, my son."

When he had gone, Prince Corum returned his attention to his music, but he found that it was difficult for him to concentrate. His imagination began to focus on the quest he had agreed to undertake. A certain emotion took hold of him. He believed that it must be excitement. When he embarked on the quest, it would be the first time in his life that he had left the environs of Castle Erorn.

He attempted to calm himself, for it was against the customs of his people to allow an excess of emotion.

"It will be instructive," he murmured to himself, "to see the rest of this continent. I wish that geography had interested me more. I scarcely know the outlines of Bro-an-Vadhagh, let alone the rest of the world. Perhaps I should study some of the maps and travelers' tales in the library. Yes, I will go there tomorrow, or perhaps the next day."

No sense of urgency filled Prince Corum, even now. The Vadhagh being a long-lived people, they were used to acting at leisure, considering their actions before performing them, spending weeks or months in meditation before embarking on some study or creative work.

Prince Corum then decided to abandon his symphony on which he had been working for the past four years. Perhaps he would take it up again on his return, perhaps not. It was of no great consequence.

PRINCE CORUM SETS FORTH

AND SO, WITH the hoofs of his horse hidden by the white mist of the morning, Prince Corum rode out from Castle Erorn to begin his quest.

The pale light softened the lines of the castle so that it seemed, more than ever, to merge with the great high rock on which it stood, and the trees that grew beside the path down which Corum rode also appeared to melt and mingle with the mist so that the landscape was a silent vision of gentle golds and greens and greys tinged with the pink rays of a distant, hidden sun. And, from beyond the rock, the sea, cloaked by the mist, could be heard retreating from the shore.

As Corum reached the sweet-smelling pines and birches of the forest a wren began to sing, was answered by the croak of a rook, and both fell silent as if startled by the sounds their own throats had made.

Corum rode on through the forest until the whisper of the sea dimmed behind him and the mist began to give way before the warming light of the rising sun. This ancient forest was familiar to him and he loved it, for it was here he had ridden as a boy and had been taught the obsolete art of war which had been considered by his father as useful a way as any of making his body strong and quick. Here, too, he had lain through whole days watching the small animals that inhabited the forest—the tiny horselike beast of grey and yellow which had a horn growing from its forehead and was no bigger than a dog; the fan-winged gloriously coloured bird that could soar higher than the eye could see and yet which built its nests in abandoned fox and badger sets underground; the large, gentle pig with thick, curly black hair that fed on moss; and many others.

Prince Corum realized that he had almost forgotten the pleasures of the forest, he had spent so long inside the castle. A small smile touched his lips as he looked about him. The forest, he thought, would endure for ever. Something so beautiful could not die.

But this thought put him, for some reason, in a melancholy mood and he urged his horse to a somewhat faster gait.

The horse was glad to gallop as fast as Corum desired, for it also knew the forest and was enjoying the exercise. It was a red Vadhagh horse with a blue-black mane and tail and it was strong, tall and graceful, unlike the shaggy, wild ponies that inhabited the forest. It was mantled in yellow velvet and hung about with panniers, two spears, a plain round shield made of different thicknesses of timber, brass, leather and silver, a long bone bow and a quiver holding a good quantity of arrows. In one of the panniers were provisions for the journey, and in another were books and maps for guidance and entertainment.

Prince Corum himself wore a conical silver helm which had his full name carved in three characters above the short peak—

Corum Jhaelen Irsei—which meant Corum, the Prince in the Scarlet Robe. It was the custom of the Vadhagh to choose a robe of distinctive colour and identify themselves by means of it, as the Nhadragh used crests and banners of greater complication. Corum wore the robe now. It had long, wide sleeves, a full skirt that was spread back over his horse's rump, and it was open at the front. At the shoulders was fixed a hood large enough to go over his helmet. It had been made from the fine, thin skin of a creature that was thought to dwell in another plane, forgotten even by the Vadhagh. Beneath the coat was a double byrnie made up of a million tiny links. The upper layer of this byrnie was silver and the lower layer was of brass.

For weapons other than bow and lance, Corum bore a long-hafted Vadhagh war-axe of delicate and intricate workmanship, a long, strong sword of a nameless metal manufactured on a different plane of the Earth, with pommel and guard worked in silver and both red and black onyx. His shirt was of blue samite and his breeks and boots were of soft brushed leather, as was his saddle, which was finished in silver.

From beneath his helm, some of Prince Corum's fine, silvery hair escaped and his youthful face now bore an expression that was half introspection, half excited anticipation at the prospect of his first sight of the ancient lands of his kinfolk.

He rode alone because none of the castle's retainers could be spared, and he rode on horseback rather than in a carriage because he wished to make the fastest possible speed.

It would be days before he would reach the first of the several castles he must visit, but he tried to imagine how different these dwelling places of his kinfolk would be and how the people themselves would strike him. Perhaps he would even find a wife among them. He knew that, while his father had not mentioned this, it had been an extra consideration in Prince Khlonskey's mind when the old man had begged him to go on this mission.

Soon Corum had left the forest and had reached the great plain called Broggfythus where once the Vadhagh and the Nhadragh had met in bloody and mystical battle.

It had been the last battle ever fought between the two races and, at its height, it had raged through all five planes. Producing neither victor nor defeated, it had destroyed more than two thirds of each of their races. Corum had heard that there were many empty castles across Bro-an-Vadhagh now, and many empty cities in the Nhadragh Isles which lay across the water from Castle Erorn.

Towards the middle of the day Corum found himself in the centre of Broggfythus and he came to the spot that marked the boundaries of the territories he had roamed as a boy. Here was the weed-grown wreckage of the vast Sky City that, during the month-long battle of his ancestors, had careered from one plane to another, rupturing the fine fabric that divided the different dimensions of the Earth until, crashing at last upon the gathered ranks of the Vadhagh and the Nhadragh, it had destroyed them. Being of a different plane, the tangled metal and stone of the Sky City still retained that peculiar shifting effect. Now it had the appearance of a mirage, though the weeds, gorse and birch trees that twined around it looked solid enough.

On other, less urgent, occasions, Prince Corum had enjoyed shifting his perspective out of this plane and into another, to see different aspects of the city, but the effort took too much energy these days and at the present moment the diaphanous wreckage represented nothing more than an obstacle around which he was forced to make various detours, for it stretched in a circumference of more than twenty miles.

But at last he reached the edge of the plain called Broggfythus and the sun set and he left behind him the world he knew and rode on towards the south-west, into lands he knew only from the maps he carried.

He rode steadily for three more days without pause until the red horse showed signs of tiredness and, in a little valley through which a cold stream flowed, he made camp and rested for a while.

Corum ate a slice of the light, nourishing bread of his people and sat with his back against the bole of an old oak while his horse cropped the grass of the river bank.

Corum's silver helm lay beside him, together with his axe and sword. He breathed the leafy air and relaxed as he contemplated the peaks of the mountains, blue, grey and white in the distance. This was pleasant, peaceful country and he was enjoying his journey through it. Once, he knew, it had been inhabited by several Vadhagh estates, but there was no trace of them now. It was as if they had grown into the landscape or been engulfed by it. Once or twice he had seen strangely shaped rocks where Vadhagh castles had stood, but they had been no more than rocks. It occurred to him that these rocks were the transmogrified remains of Vadhagh dwellings, but his intellect rejected such an impossibility. Such imaginings were the stuff of poetry, not of reason.

He smiled at his own foolishness and settled himself more comfortably against the tree. In another three days he would be at Castle Crachah, where his aunt the Princess Lorim lived. He watched as his horse folded its legs and lay down beneath the trees to sleep and he wrapped his scarlet coat about him, raised the hood and slept also.

3

THE MABDEN HERD

TOWARDS THE MIDDLE of the following morning Prince Corum was awakened by sounds that somehow did not fit the forest. His horse had heard them too, for it was up and sniffing at the air, showing small signs of agitation.

Corum frowned and went to the cool water of the river to wash his face and hands. He paused, listening again. A thump. A rattle. A clank. He thought he heard a voice shouting further down the valley and he peered in that direction and thought he saw something moving.

Corum strode back to where he had left his gear and he picked up his helmet, settling it on his head, fixed his sword's scabbard to his belt, looped the axe onto his back. Then he began to saddle the horse as it lapped the river.

The sounds were stronger now and, for some reason, Corum felt disquiet touch his mind. He mounted his horse but continued to watch.

Up the valley came a tide of beasts and vehicles. Some of the creatures were clothed in iron, fur and leather. Corum guessed that this was a Mabden herd. From the little he had read of Mabden habits, he knew the breed to be for the most part a migratory species, constantly on the move; as it exhausted one area it would move on, seeking fresh game and wild crops. He was surprised to note how much like Vadhagh arms and armour were the swords, shields and helmets worn by some of the Mabden.

Closer they came and still Corum observed them with intense curiosity, as he would study any unusual beast he had not previously seen.

This was a large group, riding in barbarically decorated chariots of timber and beaten bronze, drawn by shaggy horses with harness of leather painted in dull reds, yellows and blues. Behind the chariots came wagons, some open and some with awnings. Perhaps these carried females, Corum thought, for there were no females to be seen elsewhere.

The Mabden had thick, dirty beards, long sweeping moustaches and matted hair flowing out from under their helmets. As they moved, they yelled at each other and passed wineskins from hand to hand. Astonished, Corum recognized the language as the common tongue of the Vadhagh and the Nhadragh, though much corrupted and harshened. So the Mabden had learned a sophisticated form of speech.

Again came the unaccountable sense of disquiet. Corum backed his horse into the shadows of the trees, continuing to watch.

And now he could see why so many of the helmets and weapons were familiar.

They were Vadhagh helmets and Vadhagh weapons.

Corum frowned. Had these been looted from some old abandoned Vadhagh castle? Were they gifts? Or had they been stolen?

The Mabden also bore arms and armour of their own crude manufacture, obviously copies of Vadhagh workmanship, as well as a few Nhadragh artifacts. A few had clothes of stolen samite and linen, but for the most part they wore wolfskin cloaks, bearskin hoods, sealskin jerkins and breeks, sheepskin jackets, goatskin caps, rabbitskin kilts, pigskin boots, shirts of deerskin or wool. Some had chains of gold, bronze and iron hanging round their necks or wound about their arms or legs, or even woven into their filthy hair.

Now, as Corum watched, they began to pass him. He stifled a cough as their smell reached his nose. Many were so drunk they were almost falling out of their chariots. The heavy wheels rumbled and the hoofs of the horses plodded on. Corum saw that the wagons did not contain females, but booty. Much of it was Vadhagh treasure, there was no mistaking it.

The evidence was impossible to interpret in any other way. This was a party of warriors—a raiding party or a looting party, Corum could not be sure. But he found it hard to accept that these creatures had lately done battle with Vadhagh warriors and won.

Now the last chariots of the caravan began to pass and Corum saw that a few Mabden walked behind, tied to the chariots by ropes attached to their hands. These Mabden bore no weapons and were hardly clothed at all. They were thin, their feet were bare and bleeding, they moaned and cried out from time to time. Often the response of the charioteer to whose chariot they were attached would be to curse or laugh and tug at the ropes to make them stumble.

One did stumble and fall and desperately tried to regain his feet as he was dragged along. Corum was horrified. Why did the Mabden treat their own species in such a way? Even the

Nhadragh, who were counted more cruel than the Vadhagh, had not caused such pain to their Vadhagh prisoners in the old days.

"These are peculiar brutes, in truth," mused Corum, half-aloud.

One of the Mabden at the head of the caravan called out loudly and brought his chariot to a halt beside the river. The other chariots and wagons began to stop. Corum saw that they intended to make camp here.

Fascinated, he continued to observe them, stock-still on his horse, hidden by the trees.

The Mabden removed the yokes from the horses and led them to the water. From the wagons they took cooking pots and poles and began to build fires.

By sunset they were eating, though their prisoners, still tied to the chariots, were given nothing.

When they were done with eating, they began to drink again and soon more than half the herd was insensible, sprawled on the grass and sleeping where they fell. Others were rolling about on the ground engaged in mock fights, many of which increased in savagery so that knives and axes were drawn and some blood spilled.

The Mabden who had originally called for the caravan to stop roared at the fighting men and began to stagger among them, a wineskin clutched in one hand, kicking them and plainly ordering them to stop. Two refused to heed him and he drew the huge bronze war-axe from his belt and smashed it down on the skull of the nearest man, splitting his helmet and his head. A silence came to the camp and Corum, with an effort, made out the words the leader spoke.

"By the Dog! I'll have no more squabbling of this sort. Why spend your energies on each other? There is sport to be had yonder!" He pointed with his axe to the prisoners who were now sleeping.

A few of the Mabden laughed and nodded and rose up, moving through the faint light of the evening to where their prisoners lay. They kicked them awake, cut the ropes attached to the chariots and forced them towards the main encampment where the warriors who had not succumbed to the wine were arranging themselves in a circle. The prisoners were pushed into the centre of this circle and stood there staring in terror at the warriors.

The leader stepped into the circle and confronted the prisoners.

"When we took you with us from your village I promised you that we Denledhyssi hated only one thing more than we hated Shefanhow. Do you remember what that was?"

One of the prisoners mumbled, staring at the ground. The Mabden leader moved quickly, pushing the head of his axe under the man's chin and lifting it up.

"Aye, you have learned your lesson well, friend. Say it again."

The prisoner's tongue was thick in his mouth. His broken lips moved again and he turned his eyes to the darkening skies and tears fell down his cheeks and he yelled in a wild, cracked voice, "Those who lick Shefanhow urine!"

And a great groan shuddered from him and then he screamed.

The Mabden leader smiled, drew back his axe and rammed the haft into the man's stomach so that the scream was cut short and he doubled over in agony.

Corum had never witnessed such cruelty and his frown deepened as he saw the Mabden begin to tie down their prisoners, staking them out on the ground and bringing brands and knives to their limbs, burning and cutting them so that they did not die but writhed in pain.

The leader laughed as he watched, taking no part in the torture itself.

"Oh, your spirits will remember me as they mingle with the

Shefanhow demons in the Pits of the Dog!" he chuckled. "Oh, they will remember the Earl of the Denledhyssi, Glandyth-a-Krae, the Doom of the Shefanhow!"

Corum found it difficult to work out what these words meant. *Shefanhow* could be a corruption of the Vadhagh word *Sefano* which roughly meant 'fiend'. But why did these Mabden call themselves "Denledhyssi"—a corruption, almost certainly, of *Donledyssi* meaning 'murderers'? Were they proud that they were killers? And was *Shefanhow* a term used in general to describe their enemies? And were, as seemed unquestionably the case, their enemies other Mabden?

Corum shook his head in puzzlement. He understood the motives and behaviour of less developed animals better than he understood the Mabden. He found it difficult to retain a clinical interest in their customs, was becoming quickly disturbed by them. He turned his horse into the depths of the forest and rode away.

The only explanation he could find, at present, was that the Mabden species had undergone a process of evolution and devolution more rapid than most. It was possible that these were the mad remnants of the race. If so, then that was why they turned on their own kind, as rabid foxes did.

A greater sense of urgency filled him now and he rode as fast as his horse could gallop, heading for Castle Crachah. Princess Lorim, living in closer proximity to Mabden herds, might be able to give him clearer answers to his questions.

THE BANE OF BEAUTY:
THE DOOM OF TRUTH

S AVE FOR DEAD fires and some litter, Prince Corum saw no further signs of Mabden before he breasted the high green hills that enclosed Valley Crachah and searched with his eyes for the castle of Princess Lorim.

The valley was full of poplars, elms and birch and looked peaceful in the gentle light of the early afternoon. But where was the castle, he wondered.

Corum drew his map again from within his byrnie and consulted it. The castle should be almost in the centre of the valley, surrounded by six rings of poplars and two outer rings of elms. He looked again.

Yes, there were the rings of poplars and elms. And near the centre, no castle, just a cloud of mist.

But there should be no mist on such a day. It could only be smoke.

Prince Corum rode rapidly down the hill.

He rode until he reached the first of the rings of trees and he peered through the other rings but could, as yet, see nothing. He sniffed the smoke.

He passed through more rings of trees and now the smoke stung his eyes and throat and he could see a few black shapes in it.

He passed through the final ring of poplars and he began to choke as the smoke filled his lungs and his watering eyes made out the shapes. Sharp crags, tumbled rocks, blistered metal, burned beams.

Prince Corum saw a ruin. It was without a doubt the ruin of Castle Crachah. A smouldering ruin. Fire had brought Castle Crachah down. Fire had eaten her folk, for now Corum, as he rode his snorting horse around the perimeter of the ruins, made out blackened skeletons. And beyond the ruins were signs of battle. A broken Mabden chariot. Some Mabden corpses. An old Vadhagh woman, chopped into several pieces.

Even now the crows and ravens were beginning to sidle in, risking the smoke.

Prince Corum began to understand what sorrow must be. He thought that the emotion he felt was that.

He called out once, in the hope that some inhabitant of Castle Crachah lived, but there was no reply. Slowly, Prince Corum turned away.

He rode towards the east. Towards Castle Sarn.

He rode steadily for a week and the sense of sorrow remained but was joined by another nagging emotion. Prince Corum began to think it must be a feeling of trepidation.

Castle Sarn lay in the middle of a dense elder forest and was reached by a pathway down which the weary Prince in the

Scarlet Robe and his weary horse moved. Small animals scampered away from them and a thin rain fell from a brooding sky. No smoke rose here. And when Corum came to the castle he saw that it was no longer burning. Its black stones were cold and the crows and ravens had already picked the corpses clean and gone away in search of other carrion.

And then tears came to Corum's eyes for the first time and he dismounted from his dusty horse and clambered over the stones and the bones and sat down and looked about him.

For several hours Prince Corum sat thus until a sound came from his throat. It was a sound he had not heard before and he could not name it. It was a thin sound that could not express what was within his stunned mind. He had never known Prince Opash, though his father had spoken of him with great affection. He had never known the family and retainers who had dwelt in Castle Sarn. But he wept for them until at length, exhausted, he stretched out upon the broken slab of stone and fell into a gloomy slumber.

The rain continued to fall on Corum's scarlet coat. It fell on the ruins and it washed the bones. The red horse sought the shelter of the elder trees and lay down. For a while it chewed the grass and watched its prone master. Then it, too, slept.

When he eventually awoke and clambered back over the ruins to where his horse still lay, Corum's mind was incapable of speculation. He knew now that this destruction must be Mabden work, for it was not the custom of the Nhadragh to burn the castles of their enemies. Besides, the Nhadragh and the Vadhagh had been at peace for centuries. Both had forgotten how to make war.

It had occurred to Corum that the Mabden might have been inspired to their destruction by the Nhadragh, but even this was unlikely. There was an ancient code of war to which both races had, no matter how fierce the fighting, always adhered. And with the decline in their numbers, there had been no need for the Nhadragh to expand their territories or for the Vadhagh to defend theirs.

His face thin with weariness and strain, coated with dust and streaked with tears, Prince Corum aroused his horse and mounted him, riding on towards the north, where Castle Gal lay. He hoped a little. He hoped that the Mabden herds moved only in the south and east, that the north would still be free of their encroachments, as the west was.

A day later, as he stopped to water his horse at a small lake, he looked across the gorse moor and saw more smoke curling. He took out his map and consulted it. No castle was marked there.

He hesitated. Was the smoke coming from another Mabden camp? If so, they might have Vadhagh prisoners whom Corum should attempt to rescue. He decided to ride towards the source of the smoke.

The smoke came from several sources. This was, indeed, a Mabden camp, but it was a permanent camp, not unlike the smaller settlements of the Nhadragh, though much cruder. A collection of stone huts built close to the ground, with thatched roofs and chimneys of slate from which the smoke came.

Around this camp were fields that had evidently contained crops, though there were no crops now, and others which had a few cows grazing in them.

For some reason Corum did not feel wary of this camp as he had felt wary of the Mabden caravan, but he nonetheless approached it cautiously, stopping his horse a hundred yards away and studying the camp for signs of life.

He waited an hour and saw none.

He moved his horse in closer until he was less than fifty yards away from the nearest single-storey building.

Still no Mabden emerged from any of the low doorways.

Corum cleared his throat.

A child began to scream and the scream was muffled suddenly.

"Mabden!" Corum called, and his voice was husky with weariness and sorrow. "I would speak with you. Why do you not come out of your dens?"

From a nearby hovel a voice replied. The voice was a mixture of fear and anger.

"We have done no harm to the Shefanhow. They have done no harm to us. But if we speak to you the Denledhyssi will come back and take more of our food, kill more of our menfolk, rape more of our women. Go away, Shefanhow lord, we beg you. We have put the food in the sack by the door. Take it and leave us."

Corum saw the sack now. So, it had been an offering to him. Did they not know that their heavy food would not settle in a Vadhagh stomach?

"I do not want food, Mabden," he called back.

"What do you want, Shefanhow lord? We have nothing else but our souls."

"I do not know what you mean. I seek answers to questions."

"The Shefanhow know everything. We know nothing."

"Why do you fear the Denledhyssi? Why do you call me a fiend? We Vadhagh have never harmed you."

"The Denledhyssi call you Shefanhow. And because we dwelt in peace with your folk, the Denledhyssi punish us. They say that Mabden must kill the Shefanhow—the Vadhagh and the

Nhadragh—that you are evil. They say our crime is to let evil live. They say that the Mabden are put upon this earth to destroy the Shefanhow. The Denledhyssi are the servants of the great Earl, Glandyth-a-Krae, whose own liege is our liege, King Lyr-a-Brode whose stone city called Kalenwyr is in the high lands of the north-east. Do you not know all this, Shefanhow lord?"

"I did not know it," said Prince Corum softly, turning his horse away. "And now that I know it, I do not understand it." He raised his voice. "Farewell, Mabden, I'll give you no further cause for fear…" And then he paused. "But tell me one last thing."

"What is that, lord?" came the nervous voice.

"Why does a Mabden destroy another Mabden?"

"I do not understand you, lord."

"I have seen members of your race killing fellow members of that race. Is this something you often do?"

"Aye, lord. We do it quite often. We punish those who break our laws. We set an example to those who might consider breaking those laws."

Prince Corum sighed. "Thank you, Mabden. I ride away now."

The red horse trotted off over the moor, leaving the village behind.

Now Prince Corum knew that Mabden power had grown greater than any Vadhagh would have suspected. They had a primitively complicated social order, with leaders of different ranks. Permanent settlements of a variety of sizes. The larger part of Bro-an-Vadhagh seemed ruled by a single man—King Lyr-a-Brode. The name meant something like, in their coarsened dialect, King of All the Land.

Corum remembered the rumours. That Vadhagh castles had been taken by these half-beasts. That the Nhadragh Isles had fallen completely to them.

And there were Mabden who devoted their whole lives to seeking out members of the older races and destroying them. Why? The older races did not threaten Man. What threat could they be to a species so numerous and fierce? All that the Vadhagh and the Nhadragh had was knowledge. Was it knowledge that the Mabden feared?

For ten days, pausing twice to rest, Prince Corum rode north, but now he had a different vision of what Castle Gal would look like when he reached it. But he must go there to make sure. And he must warn Prince Faguin and his family of their danger, if they still lived.

The settlements of the Mabden were seen often and Prince Corum avoided them. Some were the size of the first he had seen, but many were larger, built around grim stone towers. Sometimes he saw bands of warriors riding by and only the sharper senses of the Vadhagh enabled him to see them before they sighted him.

Once, by a huge effort, he was forced to move both himself and his horse into the next dimension to avoid confrontation with Mabden. He watched them ride past him, less than ten feet away, completely unable to observe him. Like the others he had seen, these did not ride horses, but had chariots drawn by shaggy ponies. As Corum saw their faces, pocked with disease, thick with grease and filth, their bodies strung with barbaric ornament, he wondered at their powers of destruction. It was still hard to believe that such insensitive beasts as these, who appeared to have no second sight at all, could bring to ruin the great castles of the Vadhagh.

And at last the Prince in the Scarlet Robe reached the bottom of the hill on which Castle Gal stood and saw the black smoke billowing and the red flames leaping and knew from what fresh destruction the Mabden beasts had been riding.

But here there had been a much longer siege, by the look of it. A battle had raged here that had lasted many days. The Vadhagh had been more prepared at Castle Gal. Hoping that he would find some wounded kinsmen whom he could help, Corum urged his horse to gallop up the hill.

But the only thing that lived beyond the blazing castle was a groaning Mabden, abandoned by his fellows. Corum ignored him.

He found three corpses of his own folk. Not one of the three had died quickly or without what the Mabden would doubtless consider humiliation. There were two warriors who had been stripped of their arms and armour. And there was a child. A girl of about six years.

Corum bent and picked up the corpses one by one, carrying them to the fire to be consumed. He went to his horse.

The wounded Mabden called out. Corum paused. It was not the usual Mabden accent.

"Help me, master!"

This was the liquid tongue of the Vadhagh and the Nhadragh.

Was this a Vadhagh who had disguised himself as a Mabden to escape death? Corum began to walk back, leading his horse through the billowing smoke.

He looked down at the Mabden. He wore a bulky wolfskin coat covered by a half-byrnie of iron links, a helmet that covered most of his face and which had slipped to blind him. Corum tugged at the helmet until it was free, tossed it aside and then gasped.

This was no Mabden. Nor was it a Vadhagh. It was the bloodied face of a Nhadragh, dark with flat features and hair growing down to the ridge of the eye-sockets.

"Help me, master," said the Nhadragh again. "I am not too badly hurt. I can still be of service."

"To whom, Nhadragh?" said Corum softly. He tore off a piece

of the man's sleeve and wiped the blood free of the eyes. The Nhadragh blinked, focusing on him.

"Who would you serve, Nhadragh? Would you serve me?"

The Nhadragh's dazed eyes cleared and then filled with an emotion Corum could only surmise was hatred.

"*Vadhagh!*" snarled the being. "A Vadhagh lives!"

"Aye. I live. Why do you hate me?"

"All Nhadragh hate the Vadhagh. They have hated them through eternity! Why are you not dead? Have you been hiding?"

"I am not from Castle Gal."

"So I was right. This was not the last Vadhagh castle." The being tried to stir, tried to draw his knife, but he was too weak. He fell back.

"Hatred was not what the Nhadragh had once," Corum said. "You wanted our lands, yes. But you fought us without this *hatred*, and we fought you without it. You have learned hatred from the Mabden, Nhadragh, not from your ancestors. They knew honour. You did not. How could one of the older races make himself a Mabden slave?"

The Nhadragh's lips smiled slightly. "All the Nhadragh that remain are Mabden slaves and have been for two hundred years. They only suffer us to live in order to use us like dogs, to sniff out those beings they call Shefanhow. We swore oaths of loyalty to them in order to continue living."

"But could you not escape? There are other planes."

"The other planes were denied to us. Our historians had it that the last great battle of the Vadhagh and the Nhadragh so disrupted the equilibrium of those planes that they were closed to us by the gods…"

"So you have relearned superstition, too," mused Corum. "Ah, what do these Mabden do to us?"

The Nhadragh began to laugh and the laugh turned into a cough and blood came out of his mouth and poured down his chin. As Corum wiped away the blood, he said, "They supersede us, Vadhagh. They bring the darkness and they bring the terror. They are the bane of beauty and the doom of truth. The world is Mabden now. We have no right to continue existing. Nature abhors us. We should not be here!"

Corum sighed. "Is that your thinking, or theirs?"

"It is a fact."

Corum shrugged. "Perhaps."

"It is a fact, Vadhagh. You would be mad if you denied it."

"You said you thought this the last of our castles…"

"Not I. I sensed there was another one. I told them."

"And they have gone to seek it?"

"Yes."

Corum gripped the being's shoulder. "Where?"

The Nhadragh smiled. "Where? Where else but in the west?"

Corum ran to his horse.

"Stay!" croaked the Nhadragh. "Slay me, I pray you, Vadhagh! Do not let me linger!"

"I do not know how to kill," Corum replied as he mounted the horse.

"Then you must learn, Vadhagh. You must learn!" rasped the dying being as Corum frantically forced his horse to gallop down the hill.

5

A LESSON LEARNED

AND HERE WAS Castle Erorn, her tinted towers entwined with greedy fires. And still the surf boomed in the great black caverns within the headland on which Erorn was raised and it seemed that the sea protested, that the wind wailed its anger, that the lashing foam sought desperately to drench the victorious flame.

Castle Erorn shuddered as she perished and the bearded Mabden laughed at her downfall, shaking the brass-and-gold trappings of their chariots, casting triumphant glances at the little row of corpses lying in a semi-circle before them.

They were Vadhagh corpses.

Four women and seven men.

In the shadows on the far side of the natural bridge of rock that led to the headland, Corum saw glimpses of the bloody faces and he knew them all: Prince Khlonskey, his father. Colatalarna, his mother. His twin sisters, Ilastru and Pholhinra. His uncle, Prince Rhanan. Sertreda, his cousin. And the five retainers, all second and third cousins.

Three times Corum counted the corpses as the cold grief transformed itself to fury and he heard the butchers yell to one another in their coarse dialect.

Three times he counted, and then he looked at them and his face really was the face of a Shefanhow.

Prince Corum had discovered sorrow and he had discovered fear. Now he discovered rage.

For two weeks he had ridden almost without pause, hoping to get ahead of the Denledhyssi and warn his family of the barbarians' coming. And he had arrived a few hours too late.

The Mabden had ridden out in their arrogance born of ignorance and destroyed those whose arrogance was born of wisdom. It was the way of things. Doubtless Corum's father, Prince Khlonskey, had thought as much as he was hacked down with a stolen Vadhagh war-axe. But now Corum could find no such philosophy within his own heart.

His eyes turned black with anger, save for the irises, which turned bright gold, and he drew his tall spear and urged his weary horse over the causeway, through the flamelit night, towards the Denledhyssi.

They were lounging in their chariots and pouring sweet Vadhagh wine down their faces and into their gullets. The sounds of the sea and the blaze hid the sound of Corum's approach until his spear pierced the face of a Denledhyssi warrior and the man shrieked.

Corum had learned how to kill.

He slid the spear point free and struck the dead man's companion through the back of the neck as he began to pull himself upright. He twisted the spear.

Corum had learned how to be cruel.

Another Denledhyssi raised a bow and pulled back an arrow on the string, but Corum hurled the spear now and it struck through the man's bronze breastplate, entered his heart and knocked him over the side of the chariot.

Corum drew his second spear.

But his horse was failing him. He had ridden it to the point of exhaustion and now it could barely respond to his signals. Already the more distant charioteers were whipping their ponies into life, turning the great, groaning chariots around to bear down on the Prince in the Scarlet Robe.

An arrow passed close and Corum sought the archer and urged his tired horse forward to get close enough to drive his spear through the archer's unprotected right eye and slip it out in time to block a blow from his comrade's sword.

The metal-shod spear turned the blade and, using both hands, Corum reversed the spear to smash the butt into the swordsman's face and knock him out of the chariot.

But now the other chariots were bearing down on him through the tumbling shadows cast by the roaring fires that ate at Castle Erorn.

They were led by one whom Corum recognized. He was laughing and yelling and whirling his huge war-axe about his head.

"By the Dog! Is this a Vadhagh who knows how to fight like a Mabden? You have learned too late, my friend. You are the last of your race!"

It was Glandyth-a-Krae, his grey eyes gleaming, his cruel mouth snarling back over yellow fangs.

Corum flung his spear.

The whirling axe knocked it aside and Glandyth's chariot did not falter.

Corum unslung his own war-axe and waited and, as he

waited, the legs of his horse buckled and the beast collapsed to the ground.

Desperately Corum untangled his feet from the stirrups, gripped his axe in both hands and leapt backwards and aside as the chariot came at him. He aimed a blow at Glandyth-a-Krae, but struck the brass edge of the chariot. The shock of the blow numbed his hands so that he almost dropped the axe. He was breathing harshly now and staggered. Other chariots raced by on both sides and a sword struck his helmet. Dazed, he fell to one knee. A spear hit his shoulder and he fell in the churned mud.

Then Corum learned cunning. Instead of attempting to rise, he lay where he had fallen until all the chariots had passed. Before they could begin to turn, he pulled himself to his feet. His shoulder was bruised, but the spear had not pierced it. He stumbled through the darkness, seeking to escape the barbarians.

Then his feet struck something soft and he glanced down and saw the body of his mother and he saw what had been done to her before she died and a great moan escaped him and tears blinded him and he took a firmer grip on the axe in his left hand and painfully drew his sword, screaming, "Glandyth-a-Krae!"

And Corum had learned the lust for revenge.

The ground shook as the hoofs of the horses beat upon it, hauling the returning chariots towards him. The tall tower of the castle suddenly cracked and crumbled into the flames which leapt higher and brightened the night to show Earl Glandyth whipping the horses as he bore down on Corum once again.

Corum stood over the corpse of his mother, the gentle Princess Colatalarna. His first blow split the forehead of the leading horse and it fell, dragging the others down with it.

Earl Glandyth was flung forward, almost over the edge of the chariot, and he cursed. Behind him two other charioteers hastily tried to rein in their horses to stop from crashing into their leader. The others, not understanding why they were stopping, also hauled at their reins.

Corum clambered over the bodies of the horses and swung his sword at Glandyth's neck, but the blow was blocked by a gorget and the huge, hairy head turned and the pale grey eyes glared at Corum. Then Glandyth leapt from the chariot and Corum leapt too, to come face to face with the destroyer of his family.

They confronted each other in the firelight, panting like foxes, crouching and ready to spring.

Corum moved first, lunging with his sword at Glandyth-a-Krae and swinging his axe at the same time.

Glandyth jumped away from the sword and used his own axe to parry the blow, kicking out at Corum's groin, but missing.

They began to circle, Corum's black-and-gold eyes locked on the pale grey ones of the Mabden earl.

For several minutes they circled, while the other Mabden looked on. Glandyth's lips moved and began to voice a word, but Corum sprang in again and this time the alien metal of his slender sword pierced Glandyth's armour at the shoulder join and slid in. Glandyth hissed and his axe swung round to strike the sword with such a blow that it was wrenched from Corum's aching hand and fell to the ground.

"Now," murmured Glandyth, as if speaking to himself. "Now, Vadhagh. It is not my fate to be slain by a Shefanhow."

Corum swung his axe.

Again Glandyth dodged the blow.

Again his axe came down.

And this time Corum's weapon was struck from his hand and he stood defenseless before the grinning Mabden.

"But it is my fate to slay Shefanhow!" He twisted his mouth in a snarling grin.

Corum flung himself at Glandyth, trying to wrest the axe from him. But Corum had spent the last of his strength. He was too weak.

Glandyth cried out to his men. "By the Dog, lads, get this demon off me. Do not slay him. We'll take our time with him. After all, he is the last Vadhagh we shall ever have the chance to sport with!"

Corum heard them laugh and he struck out at them as they seized him. He was shouting as a man shouts in a fever and he could not hear the words.

Then one Mabden plucked off his silver helm and another hit him on the back of the head with a sword pommel and Corum's body went suddenly limp and sank down into welcome darkness.

6

THE MAIMING OF CORUM

THE SUN HAD risen and set twice before Corum awoke to
find himself trussed in chains in the back of a Mabden
wagon. He tried to raise his head and see through the gap
in the awning, but he saw nothing, save that it was daytime.

Why had they not killed him? he wondered. And then he
shuddered as he understood that they were waiting for him to
awake so that they could make his death both long and painful.

Before he had set off on his quest, before he had witnessed
what had happened to the Vadhagh castles, before he had seen
the blight that had come to Bro-an-Vadhagh, he might have
accepted his fate and prepared himself to die as his kinfolk had
died, but the lessons he had learned remained with him. He hated
the Mabden. He mourned for his relatives. He would avenge
them if he could. And this meant that he would have to live.

He closed his eyes, conserving his strength. There was one
way to escape the Mabden and that was to ease his body into
another plane where they could not see him. But to do this would

49

demand much energy and there was little point in doing it while he remained in the wagon.

The guttural Mabden voices drifted back to the wagon from time to time, but he could not hear what they said. He slept.

He stirred. Something cold was striking his face. He blinked. It was water. He opened his eyes and saw the Mabden standing over him. He had been removed from the wagon and was lying on the ground. Cooking fires burned nearby. It was night.

"The Shefanhow is with us again, master," called the Mabden who had thrown the water. "He is ready for us, I think."

Corum winced as he moved his bruised body, trying to stand upright in the chains. Even if he could escape to another plane, the chains would come with him. He would be little better off. Experimentally, he tried to see into the next plane, but his eyes began to ache and he gave up.

Earl Glandyth-a-Krae appeared now, pushing his way through his men. His pale eyes regarded Corum triumphantly. He put a hand to his beard, which had been plaited into several strands and strung with rings of stolen gold, and he smiled. Almost tenderly, he reached down and pulled Corum upright. The chains and the cramped space of the wagon had served to cut off the circulation of blood to his legs. They began to buckle.

"Rodlik! Here, lad!" Earl Glandyth called behind him.

"Coming, master!" A red-headed boy of about fourteen trotted forward. He was dressed in soft Vadhagh samite, both green and white, and there was an ermine cap on his head, soft deerskin boots on his feet. He had a pale face, spotted with acne, but otherwise handsome for a Mabden. He knelt before Earl Glandyth. "Aye, lord?"

"Help the Shefanhow to stand, lad." Glandyth's low, harsh voice contained something like a note of affection as he addressed the boy. "Help him stand, Rodlik."

Rodlik sprang up and took Corum's elbow, steadying him. The boy's touch was cold and nervous.

All the Mabden warriors looked expectantly at Glandyth. Casually, he took off his heavy helmet and shook out his hair which was curled and heavy with grease.

Corum, too, watched Glandyth. He studied the man's red face, decided that the grey eyes showed little real intelligence, but much malice and pride.

"Why have you destroyed all the Vadhagh?" said Corum quietly. His mouth moved painfully. "Why, Earl of Krae?"

Glandyth looked at him as if in surprise and he was slow to reply. "You should know. We hate your sorcery. We loathe your superior airs. We desire your lands and those goods of yours which are of use to us. So we kill you." He grinned. "Besides, we have not destroyed *all* the Vadhagh. Not yet. One left."

"Aye," promised Corum. "And one that will avenge his people if he is given the opportunity."

"No." Glandyth put his hands on his hips. "He will not be."

"You say you hate our sorcery. But we have no sorcery. Just a little knowledge, a little second sight…"

"Ha! We have seen your castles and the evil contraptions they contain. We saw that one, back there—the one we took a couple of nights ago. Full of sorcery!"

Corum wetted his lips. "Yet even if we did have such sorcery, that would be no reason for destroying us. We have offered you no harm. We have let you come to our land without resisting you. I think you hate us because you hate something in yourselves. You are—unfinished—creatures."

"I know. You call us half-beasts. I care not what you think now, Vadhagh. Not now that your race is gone." He spat on the ground and waved his hand at the youth. "Let him go."

The youth sprang back.

Corum swayed, but did not fall. He continued to stare in contempt at Glandyth-a-Krae.

"You and your race are insane, earl. You are like a canker. You are a sickness suffered by this world."

Earl Glandyth spat again. This time he spat straight into Corum's face. "I told you—I know what the Vadhagh think of us. I know what the Nhadragh thought before we made them our hunting dogs. Your pride has destroyed you, Vadhagh. The Nhadragh learned to do away with pride and so some of them were spared. They accepted us as their masters. But you Vadhagh could not. When we came to your castles, you ignored us. When we demanded tribute, you said nothing. When we told you that you served us now, you pretended you did not understand us. So we set out to punish you. And you would not resist. We tortured you and, in your pride, you would not give us an oath that you would be our slaves, as the Nhadragh did. We lost patience, Vadhagh. We decided that you were not fit to live in the same land as the great King Lyr-a-Brode, for you would not admit to being his subjects. That is why we set out to slay you all. You earned this doom."

Corum looked at the ground. So it was complacency that had brought down the Vadhagh race.

He lifted his head again and stared back at Glandyth.

"I hope, however," said Corum, "that I will be able to show you that the last of the Vadhagh can behave in a different way."

Glandyth shrugged and turned to address his men.

"He hardly knows what he will show us soon, does he, lads?"

The Mabden laughed.

"Prepare the board!" Earl Glandyth ordered. "I think we shall begin."

Corum saw them bring up a wide plank of wood. It was thick and pitted and stained. Near its four corners were fixed lengths of chain. Corum began to guess at the board's function.

Two Mabden grasped his arms and pushed him towards the board. Another brought a chisel and an iron hammer. Corum was pushed with his back against the board, which now rested on the trunk of a tree. Using the chisel, a Mabden struck the chains from him, then his arms and legs were seized and he was spreadeagled on the board while new rivets were driven into the links of chain securing him there. Corum could smell stale blood. He could see where the board was scored with the marks of knives, swords and axes, where arrows had been shot into it.

He was on a butcher's block.

The Mabden bloodlust was rising. Their eyes gleamed in the firelight, their breath steamed and their nostrils dilated. Red tongues licked thick lips and small, anticipatory smiles were on several faces.

Earl Glandyth had been supervising the pinning of Corum to the board. Now he came up and stood in front of the Vadhagh and he drew a slim, sharp blade from his belt.

Corum watched as the blade came towards his chest. Then there was a ripping sound as the knife tore the samite shirt away from his body.

Slowly, his grin spreading, Glandyth-a-Krae worked at the rest of Corum's clothing, the knife only occasionally drawing a thin line of blood from his body, until at last Corum was completely naked.

Glandyth stepped back.

"Now," he said, panting, "you are doubtless wondering what we intend to do with you."

"I have seen others of my people whom you have slain," Corum said. "I think I know what you intend to do."

Glandyth raised the little finger of his right hand while he tucked his dagger away with his left.

"Ah, you see. You do not know. Those other Vadhagh died swiftly—or relatively so—because we had so many to find and to kill. But you are the last. We can take our time with you. We think, in fact, that we will give you a chance to live. If you *can* survive with your eyes gone, your tongue put out, your hands and feet removed and your genitals taken away, then we will let you so survive."

Corum stared at him in horror.

Glandyth burst into laughter. "I see you appreciate our joke!"

He signaled to his men.

"Bring the tools! Let's begin."

A great brazier was brought forward. It was full of red-hot charcoal and from it poked irons of various sorts. These were instruments especially designed for torture, thought Corum. What sort of race could conceive such things and call itself sane?

Glandyth-a-Krae selected a long iron from the brazier and turned it this way and that, inspecting the glowing tip.

"We will begin with an eye and end with an eye," he said. "The right eye, I think."

If Corum had eaten anything in the last few days, he would have vomited then. As it was, bile came into his mouth and his stomach trembled and ached.

There were no further preliminaries.

Glandyth began to advance with the heated iron. It smoked in the cold night air.

Now Corum tried to forget the threat of torture and concentrate on his second sight, trying to see into the next plane. He sweated with a mixture of terror and the effort of his thought. But his mind was confused. Alternately, he saw glimpses of the next plane and the ever-advancing tip of the iron coming closer and closer to his face.

The scene before him shivered, but still Glandyth came on, the grey eyes burning with an unnatural lust.

Corum twisted in the chains, trying to avert his head. Then Glandyth's left hand shot out and tangled itself in his hair, forcing the head back, bringing the iron down.

Corum screamed as the red-hot tip touched the lid of his closed eye. Pain filled his face and then his whole body. He heard a mixture of laughter, his own shouts, Glandyth's rasping breathing...

...and Corum fainted.

Corum wandered through the streets of a strange city. The buildings were high and seemed but recently built, though already they were grimed and smeared with slime.

There was still pain, but it was remote, dull. He was blind in one eye. From a balcony a woman's voice called him. He looked around. It was his sister, Pholhinra. When she saw his face, she cried out in horror.

Corum tried to put his hand to his injured eye, but he could not.

Something held him. He tried to wrench his left hand free from whatever gripped it. He pulled harder and harder. Now the wrist began to pulse with pain as he tugged.

Pholhinra had disappeared, but Corum was now absorbed with trying to free his hand. For some reason, he could not turn to see what it was that held him. Some kind of beast, perhaps, holding onto his hand with its jaws.

Corum gave one last, huge tug and his wrist came free.

He put up the hand to touch the blind eye, but still felt nothing.

He looked at the hand.

There was no hand. Just a wrist. Just a stump.

Then he screamed again…

…and he opened his eyes and saw the Mabden holding the arm and bringing down white-hot swords on the stump to seal it.

They had cut off his hand.

And Glandyth was still laughing, holding Corum's severed hand up to show his men, with Corum's blood still dripping from the knife he had used.

Now Corum saw the other plane distinctly, superimposed, as it were, over the scene before him. Summoning all the energy born of his fear and agony, he shifted himself into that plane.

He saw the Mabden clearly, but their voices had become faint. He heard them cry out in astonishment and point at him. He saw Glandyth wheel, his eyes widening. He heard the Earl of Krae call out to his men to search the woods for Corum.

The board was abandoned as Glandyth and his men lumbered off into the darkness seeking their Vadhagh captive.

But their captive was still chained to the board, for it, like him, existed on several planes. And he still felt the pain they had caused him and he was still without his right eye and his left hand.

He could stay away from further mutilation for a little while, but eventually his energy would give out completely and he would return to their plane and they would continue their work.

He struggled in the chains, waving the stump of his left wrist in a futile attempt to free himself of those manacles still holding his other limbs.

But he knew it was hopeless. He had only averted his doom for a short while. He would never be free—never be able to exercise his vengeance on the murderer of his kin.

7

THE BROWN MAN

CORUM SWEATED AS he forced himself to remain in the other plane, and he watched nervously for the return of Glandyth and his men.

It was then that he saw a shape move cautiously out of the forest and approach the board.

At first Corum thought it was a Mabden warrior, without a helmet and dressed in a huge fur jerkin. Then he realized that this was some other creature.

The creature moved cautiously towards the board, looked about the Mabden camp, and then crept closer. It lifted its head and stared directly at Corum.

Corum was astonished. The beast could see him! Unlike the Mabden, unlike the other creatures of the plane, this one had second sight.

Corum's agony was so intense that he was forced to screw up his eye at the pain. When he opened it again, the creature had come right up to the board.

It was a beast not unlike the Mabden in general shape, but it was wholly covered in its own fur. Its face was brown and seamed and apparently very ancient. Its features were flat. It had large eyes, round like a cat's, and gaping nostrils and a huge mouth filled with old, yellowed fangs.

Yet there was a look of great sorrow on its face as it observed Corum. It gestured at him and grunted, pointing into the forest as if it wanted Corum to accompany him. He shook his head, indicating the manacles with a nod.

The creature stroked the curly brown fur of its own neck thoughtfully, then it shuffled away again, back into the darkness of the forest.

Corum watched it go, almost forgetful of his pain in his astonishment.

Had the creature witnessed his torture? Was it trying to save him?

Or perhaps this was an illusion, like the illusion of the city and his sister, induced by his agonies.

He felt his energy weakening. A few more moments and he would be returning to the plane where the Mabden would be able to see him. And he knew that he would not find the strength again to leave the plane.

Then the brown creature reappeared and it was leading something by one of its hands, pointing at Corum.

At first Corum saw only a bulky shape looming over the brown creature—a being that stood some twelve feet tall and was some six feet broad, a being that, like the furry beast, walked on two legs.

Corum looked up at it and saw that it had a face. It was a dark face and the expression on it was sad, concerned, doomed. The rest of its body, though in outline the same as a man's, seemed to refuse light—no detail of it could be observed. It reached out and it picked up the board as tenderly as a father might pick up a child. It bore Corum back with it into the forest.

Unable to decide if this were fantasy or reality, Corum gave up his efforts to remain on the other plane and merged back into the one he had left. But still the dark-faced creature carried him, the brown beast at its side, deep into the forest, moving at great speed until they were far away from the Mabden camp.

Corum fainted once again.

He awoke in daylight and he saw the board lying some distance away. He lay on the green grass of a valley and there was a spring nearby and, close to that, a little pile of nuts and fruit. Not far from the pile of food sat the brown beast. It was watching him.

Corum looked at his left arm. Something had been smeared on the stump and there was no pain there any more. He put his right hand to his right eye and touched sticky stuff that must have been the same salve as that which was on his stump.

Birds sang in the nearby woods. The sky was clear and blue. If it were not for his injuries, Corum might have thought the events of the last few weeks a black dream.

Now the brown, furry creature got up and shambled towards him. It cleared its throat. Its expression was still one of sympathy. It touched its own right eye, its own left wrist.

"How—pain?" it said in a slurred tone, obviously voicing the words with difficulty.

"Gone," Corum said. "I thank you, brown man, for your help in rescuing me."

The brown man frowned at him, evidently not understanding

all the words. Then it smiled and nodded its head and said, "Good."

"Who are you?" Corum said. "Who was it you brought last night?"

The creature tapped its chest. "Me Serwde. Me friend of you."

"Serwde," said Corum, pronouncing the name poorly. "I am Corum. And who was the other being?"

Serwde spoke a name that was far more difficult to pronounce than his own. It seemed a complicated name.

"Who was he? I have never seen a being like him. I have never seen a being like yourself, for that matter. Where do you come from?"

Serwde gestured about him. "Me live here. In forest. Forest called Laahr. My master live here. We live here many, many, many days—since before Vadhagh, you folk."

"And where is your master now?" Corum asked again.

"He gone. Not want be seen folk."

And now Corum dimly recalled a legend. It was a legend of a creature that lived even further to the west than the people of Castle Erorn. It was called by the legend the Brown Man of Laahr. And this was the legend come to life. But he remembered no legend concerning the other being whose name he could not pronounce.

"Master say place nearby will tend you good," said the Brown Man.

"What sort of place, Serwde?"

"Mabden place."

Corum smiled crookedly. "No, Serwde. The Mabden will not be kind to me."

"This different Mabden."

"All Mabden are my enemies. They hate me." Corum looked at his stump. "And I hate them."

"These *old* Mabden. *Good* Mabden."

Corum got up and staggered. Pain began to nag in his head, his left wrist began to ache. He was still completely naked and his body bore many bruises and small cuts, but it had been washed.

Slowly it began to dawn on him that he was a cripple. He had been saved from the worst of what Glandyth had planned for him, but he was now less of a being than he had been. His face was no longer pleasing for others to look at. His body had become ugly.

And the wretch that he had become was all that was left of the noble Vadhagh race. He sat down again and he began to weep.

Serwde grunted and shuffled about. He touched Corum's shoulder with one of his handlike paws. He patted Corum's head, trying to comfort him.

Corum wiped his face with his good hand. "Do not worry, Serwde. I must weep for if I did not I should almost certainly die. I weep for my kin. I am the last of my line. There are no more Vadhagh but me..."

"Serwde too. Master too," said the Brown Man of Laahr. "We have no more people like us."

"Is that why you saved me?"

"No. We helped you because Mabden were hurting you."

"Have the Mabden ever hurt you?"

"No. We hide from them. Their eyes bad. Never see us. We hide from Vadhagh, the same."

"Why do you hide?"

"My master know. We stay safe."

"It would have been well for the Vadhagh if they had hidden. But the Mabden came so suddenly. We were not warned. We left our castles so rarely, we communicated among ourselves so little, we were not prepared."

Serwde only half understood what Corum was saying, but he listened politely until Corum stopped, then he said, "You eat.

Fruit good. You sleep. Then we go to Mabden place."

"I want to find arms and armour, Serwde. I want clothes. I want a horse. I want to go back to Glandyth and follow him until I see him alone. Then I want to kill him. After that, I will wish only to die."

Serwde looked sadly at Corum. "You kill?"

"Only Glandyth. He killed my people."

Serwde shook his head. "Vadhagh not kill like that."

"I do, Serwde. I am the last Vadhagh. And I am the first to learn what it is to kill in malice. I will be avenged on those who maimed me, on those who took away my family."

Serwde grunted miserably.

"Eat. Sleep."

Corum stood up again and realized he was very weak. "Perhaps you are right there. Perhaps I should try to restore my strength before I carry on." He went to the pile of nuts and fruits and began to eat. He could not eat much at first and lay down again to sleep, confident that Serwde would rouse him if danger threatened.

For five days Corum stayed in the valley with the Brown Man of Laahr. He hoped that the dark-faced creature would come back and tell him more of his and Serwde's origin, but this did not happen.

At last his wounds had healed completely and he felt well enough to set off on a journey. On that morning, he addressed Serwde.

"Farewell, Brown Man of Laahr. I thank you for saving me. And I thank your master. Now I go."

Corum saluted Serwde and began to walk up the valley, heading towards the east. Serwde came shambling after him.

"Corum! Corum! You go wrong way."

"I go back to where I shall find my enemies," Corum said. "That is not the wrong way."

"My master say, me take you that way..." Serwde pointed towards the west.

"There is only sea that way, Serwde. It is the far tip of Bro-an-Vadhagh."

"My master say that way," insisted Serwde.

"I am grateful for your concern, Serwde. But I go this way—to find the Mabden and take my revenge."

"You go that way." Serwde pointed again and put his paw on Corum's arm. "That way."

Corum shook the paw off. "No. This way." He continued to walk up the valley towards the east.

Then, suddenly, something struck him on the back of the head. He reeled and turned to see what had struck him. Serwde stood there, holding another stone ready.

Corum cursed and was about to berate Serwde when his senses left him again and he fell full-length on the grass.

He was awakened by the sound of the sea.

At first he could not decide what was happening to him and then he realized that he was being carried, face down, over Serwde's shoulder. He struggled, but the Brown Man of Laahr was much stronger than he appeared to be. He held Corum firmly.

Corum looked to one side. There was the sea, green and foaming against the shingle. He looked to the other side, his blind side, and managed to strain his head round to see what lay there.

It was the sea again. He was being carried along a narrow piece of land that rose out of the water. Eventually, though his head was bumping up and down as Serwde jogged along, he saw that they had left the mainland and were moving along some kind of natural causeway that stretched out into the ocean.

Seabirds called. Corum shouted and struggled, but Serwde remained deaf to his curses and entreaties, until the Brown Man stopped at last and dumped him to the ground.

Corum got up.

"Serwde, I…"

He paused, looking about him.

They had come to the end of the causeway and were on an island that rose steeply from the sea. At the peak of the island was a castle of a kind of architecture Corum had never seen before.

Was this the Mabden place Serwde had spoken of?

But Serwde was already trotting back down the causeway. Corum called to him. The Brown Man only increased his pace. Corum began to follow, but he could not match the creature's speed. Serwde had reached the land long before Corum had crossed halfway—and now his path was blocked, for the tide was rising to cover the causeway.

Corum paused in indecision, looking back at the castle. Serwde's misguided help had placed him, once again, in danger.

Now he saw mounted figures coming down the steep path from the castle. They were warriors. He saw the sun flash on their lances and on their breastplates. Unlike other Mabden, these did know how to ride horses, and there was something in their bearing that made them look more like Vadhagh than Mabden.

But, nonetheless, they were enemies and Corum's choice was to face them naked or try to swim back to the mainland with only one hand.

He made up his mind and waded into the brine, the cold water making him gasp, heedless of the shouts of the riders behind him.

He managed to swim a little way until he was in deeper water, and then the current seized him. He fought to swim free of it, but it was useless.

Rapidly, he was borne out to sea.

THE MARGRAVINE OF ALLOMGLYL

ORUM HAD LOST much blood during the Mabden torturings and had by no means recovered his original strength. It was not long before he could fight the current no more and the cramps began to set in his limbs.

He began to drown.

Destiny seemed determined that he should not live to take his vengeance on Glandyth-a-Krae.

Water filled his mouth and he fought to keep it from entering his lungs as he twisted and thrashed in the water. Then he heard a shout from above and tried to peer upwards through his good eye to locate the source of the voice.

"Stay still, Vadhagh. You'll frighten my beast. They're nervous monsters at the best of times."

Now Corum saw a dark shape hovering over him. It had great wings that spread four times the length of the largest eagle's. But it was not a bird and, though its wings had a reptilian appearance, it was not a reptile. Corum recognized it for what it was. The ugly, apelike face with its white, thin fangs was the face of a gigantic bat. And the bat had a rider on it.

The rider was a lithe young Mabden who appeared to have little in common with the Mabden warriors of Glandyth-a-Krae. He was actually climbing down the side of the creature and making it flap lower so that he could extend a hand to Corum.

Corum automatically stretched out his nearest arm and realized that it was the one without a hand. The Mabden was unconcerned. He grabbed the limb near the elbow and hauled Corum up so that Corum could use his single hand to grasp a tethering strap which secured a high saddle on the back of the great bat.

Unceremoniously, Corum's dripping body was hauled up and draped in front of the rider who called something in a shrill voice and made the bat climb high above the waves and turn back in the direction of the island castle.

The beast was evidently hard to control, for the rider constantly corrected course and continued to speak to it in the high-pitched language to which it responded. But at length they had reached the island and were hovering over the castle.

Corum could hardly believe that this was Mabden architecture. There were turrets and parapets of delicate workmanship, roof-walks and balconies covered in ivy and flowers, all fashioned from a fine, white stone that shone in the sunlight.

The bat landed clumsily and the rider got off quickly, pulling Corum with him. Almost instantly, the bat was up again, wheeling in the sky and then diving towards a destination on the other side of the island.

"They sleep in caves," the rider explained. "We use them as little as possible. They're hard things to control, as you saw."

Corum said nothing.

For all that the Mabden had saved his life and seemed both

cheerful and courteous, Corum had learned, as an animal learns, that the Mabden were his enemies. He glowered at the Mabden.

"What have you saved me *for*, Mabden?"

The man looked surprised. He dusted down his tunic of scarlet velvet and adjusted his sword belt on his hips. "You were drowning," he said. "Why did you run away from our men when they came to greet you?"

"How did you know I was coming?"

"We were told by our Margravine to expect you."

"And who told your Margravine?"

"I know not. You are somewhat ungracious, sir. I thought the Vadhagh a courteous folk."

"And I thought the Mabden vicious and mad," Corum replied. "But you…"

"Ah, you speak of the folk of the south and east, eh? You have met them, then?"

With his stump, Corum tapped his ruined eye. "They did this."

The young man nodded his head sympathetically. "I suppose I would have guessed. Mutilation is one of their favourite sports. I am surprised you escaped."

"I, too."

"Well, sir," said the youth, spreading his hand in an elaborate gesture towards a doorway in a tower, "would you go in?"

Corum hesitated.

"We are not your Mabden of the east, sir, I assure you."

"Possibly," Corum said harshly, "but Mabden you are. There are so many of you. And now, I find, there are even varieties. I suspect you share common traits, however…"

The young man showed signs of impatience. "As you like, Sir Vadhagh. I, for one, will go in. I trust you will follow me at your leisure."

Corum watched him enter the doorway and disappear. He remained on the roof, watching the seabirds drift, dive and climb. With his good hand, he stroked the stump of his left wrist and shivered. A strong wind was beginning to blow and it was cold and he was naked. He glanced towards the doorway.

A woman stood there. She seemed quiet and self-contained and had a gentleness about her. Her long black hair was soft and fell to below her shoulders. She was wearing a gown of embroidered samite containing a multitude of rich colours. She smiled at him.

"Greetings," she said. "I am Rhalina. Who are you, sir?"

"I am Corum Jhaelen Irsei," he replied. Her beauty was not that of a Vadhagh, but it affected him nonetheless. "The Prince in the—"

"—Scarlet Robe?" She was plainly amused. "I speak the old Vadhagh tongue as well as the common speech. You are misnamed, Prince Corum. I see no robe. In fact, I see no…"

Corum turned away. "Do not mock me, Mabden. I am resolved to suffer no further at the hands of your kind."

She moved nearer. "Forgive me. Those who did this to you are not our kind, though they be of the same race. Have you never heard of Lywm-an-Esh?"

His brow furrowed. The name of the land was familiar, but meant nothing.

"Lywm-an-Esh," she continued, "is the name of the country whence my people come. That people is an ancient one and has lived in Lywm-an-Esh since well before the Great Battles of the Vadhagh and the Nhadragh shook the Five Planes…"

"You know of the Five Planes?"

"We once had seers who could look into them. Though their skills never matched those of the Old Folk—your folk."

"How do you know so much of the Vadhagh?"

"Though the sense of curiosity atrophied in the Vadhagh many centuries ago, ours did not," she said. "From time to time Nhadragh ships were wrecked on our shores and, though the Nhadragh themselves vanished away, books and tapestries and other artifacts were left behind. We learned to read those books and interpret those tapestries. In those days we had many scholars."

"And now?"

"Now, I do not know. We receive little news from the mainland."

"What? And it so close?"

"Not that mainland, Prince Corum," said she with a nod in the direction of the shore. She pointed out to sea. "That mainland—Lywm-an-Esh—or, more specifically, the Duchy of Bedwilral-nan-Rywm, on whose borders this Margravate once lay."

Prince Corum watched the sea as it foamed on the rocks at the base of the island. "What ignorance was ours," he mused, "when we thought we had so much wisdom."

"Why should such a race as the Vadhagh be interested in the affairs of a Mabden land?" she said. "Our history was brief and without colour compared with yours."

"But why a Margravate here?" he continued. "What do you defend your land against?"

"Other Mabden, Prince Corum."

"Glandyth and his kind."

"I know of no Glandyth. I speak of the Pony Tribes. They occupy the forests of yonder coast. Barbarians, they ever represented a threat to Lywm-an-Esh. The Margravate was made as a bastion between those tribes and our land."

"Is the sea not sufficient a bastion?"

"The sea was not here when the Margravate was established.

Once this castle stood in a forest and the sea lay miles away to the north and the south. But then the sea began to eat our land away. Every year it devours more of our cliffs. Towns, villages and castles have vanished in the space of weeks. The people of the mainland retreat ever further back into the interior…"

"And you are left behind? Has not this castle ceased to fulfill its function? Why do you not leave and join your folk?"

She smiled and shrugged, walking to the battlements and leaning out to watch the seabirds gather on the rocks. "This is my home," she said. "This is where my memories are. The Margrave left so many mementoes. I could not leave."

"The Margrave?"

"Earl Moidel of Allomglyl. My husband."

"Ah." Corum felt a strange twinge of disappointment.

The Margravine Rhalina continued to stare out to sea. "He is dead," she said. "Killed in a shipwreck. He took our last ship and set off for the mainland seeking news of the fate of our folk. A storm blew up shortly after he had gone. The ship was barely seaworthy. It sank."

Corum said nothing.

As if the Margravine's words had reminded it of its temper, the wind suddenly blew stronger, plucking at her gown and making it swirl about her body. She turned to look at him. It was a long, thoughtful stare.

"And now, prince," she said. "Will you be my guest?"

"Tell me one more thing, Lady Rhalina. How did you know of my coming? Why did the Brown Man bring me here?"

"He brought you at the behest of his master."

"And his master?"

"Told me to expect you and let you rest here until your mind and your body were healed. I was more than willing to agree. We have no visitors, normally—and certainly none of the Vadhagh race."

"But who is that strange being, the Brown Man's master? I saw him only briefly. I could not distinguish his shape too well, though I knew he was twice my size and had a face of infinite sadness."

"That is he. He comes to the castle at night, bringing sick domestic animals that have escaped our stables at some time or another. We think he is a being from another plane, or perhaps another age, before even the Age of the Vadhagh and the Nhadragh. We cannot pronounce his name, so we call him simply the Giant of Laahr."

Corum smiled for the first time. "Now I understand better. To him, perhaps, I was another sick beast. This is where he always brings sick beasts."

"You could be right, Prince Corum." She indicated the doorway. "And if you are sick, we should be happy to help you mend..."

A shadow passed over Corum's face as he followed her inside. "I fear that nothing can mend my sickness now, lady. It is a disease of the Mabden and there are no cures known to the Vadhagh."

"Well," she said with forced lightness, "perhaps we Mabden can devise something."

Bitterness filled him then. As they descended the steps into the main part of the castle he held up his stump and touched his eyeless socket. "But can the Mabden give me back my hand and eye?"

She turned and paused on the steps. She gave him an oddly candid look. "Who knows?" she said quietly. "Perhaps they can."

CONCERNING LOVE AND HATRED

ALTHOUGH DOUBTLESS MAGNIFICENT by Mabden standards, the Margravine's castle struck Prince Corum as simple and pleasant. At her invitation, he allowed himself to be bathed and oiled by castle servants and was offered a selection of clothing to wear. He chose a samite shirt of dark blue, embroidered in a design of light blue, a pair of brown linen breeks. The clothes fitted him well.

"They were the Margrave's," a girl servant told him shyly, not looking at him directly.

None of the servants had seemed at ease with him. He guessed that his appearance was repellent to them.

Reminded of this, he asked the girl, "Would you bring me a mirror?"

"Aye, lord." She ducked her head and left the chamber. But it was the Margravine herself who returned with the mirror. She did not hand it to him immediately.

"Have you not seen your face since it was injured?" she asked.

He shook his head.

"You were handsome?"

"I do not know."

She looked at him frankly. "Yes," she said. "You were handsome." Then she gave him the mirror.

The face he saw was framed by the same light golden hair, but it was no longer youthful. Fear and agony had left their marks. The face was lined and hard and the set of the mouth grim. One eye of gold and purple stared bleakly back at him. The other socket was an ugly hole made up of red, scarred tissue. There was a small scar on his left cheek and another on his neck. The face was still characteristically a Vadhagh face, but it had suffered abuse never suffered by a Vadhagh before. From the face of an angel it had been transformed by Glandyth's knives and irons into the face of a demon.

Silently, Corum gave her back the mirror.

He passed his good hand over the scars of his face and he brooded. "If I was handsome, I am ugly now."

She shrugged. "I have seen much worse."

Then the rage began to fill him again and his eye blazed and he shook the stump of his hand and he shouted at her. "Aye—and you will see much worse when I have done with Glandyth-a-Krae!"

Surprised, she recoiled from him and then regained her composure. "If you did not know you were handsome, if you were not vain, then why has this affected you so much?"

"I need my hands and my eyes so that I may kill Glandyth and watch him perish. With only half of these, I lose half the pleasure!"

"That is a childish statement, Prince Corum. It is not worthy of a Vadhagh. What else has this Glandyth done?"

Corum realized that he had not told her, that she would not

know, living in this remote place, as cut off from the world as any Vadhagh had been.

"He has slain all the Vadhagh," he said. "Glandyth has destroyed my race and would have destroyed me if it had not been for your friend, the Giant of Laahr."

"He has done what…?" Her voice was faint. She was plainly shocked.

"He has put all my folk to death."

"For what reason? Have you been warring with this Glandyth?"

"We did not know of his existence. It did not occur to us to guard against the Mabden. They seemed so much like brutes, incapable of harming us in our castles. But they have razed all our castles. Every Vadhagh save me is dead and most of the Nhadragh, I learned, who are not their cringing slaves."

"Are these the Mabden whose king is called Lyr-a-Brode of Kalenwyr?"

"They are."

"I, too, did not know they had become so powerful. I had assumed that it was the Pony Tribes who had captured you. I wondered why you were travelling alone so far from the nearest Vadhagh castle."

"What castle is that?" For a moment Corum hoped that there were Vadhagh still alive, much further west than he had guessed.

"It is called Castle Eran—Erin—some such name."

"Erorn?"

"Aye. That sounds the right name. It is over five hundred miles from here…"

"Five hundred miles? Have I come so far? The Giant of Laahr must have carried me much further than I suspected. That castle you mention, my lady, was our castle. The Mabden destroyed it. It will take me longer than I thought to return and find Earl Glandyth and his Denledhyssi."

Suddenly Corum realized just how alone he was. It was as if he had entered another plane of Earth where everything was alien to him. He knew nothing of this world. A world in which the Mabden ruled. How proud his race had been. How foolish. If only they had concerned themselves with knowledge of the world around them instead of seeking after abstractions.

Corum bowed his head.

The Margravine Rhalina seemed to understand his emotion. She lightly touched his arm. "Come, Prince of the Vadhagh. You must eat."

He allowed her to lead him from the room and into another where a meal had been laid out for them both. The food—mainly fruit and forms of edible seaweed—was much closer to his taste than any Mabden food he had seen previously. He realized that he was very hungry and that he was deeply tired. His mind was confused and his only certainty was the hatred he still felt for Glandyth and the vengeance he intended to take as soon as possible.

As they ate, they did not speak, but the Margravine watched his face the whole time and once or twice she opened her lips as if to say something, but then seemed to decide against it.

The room in which they ate was small and hung with rich tapestries covered in fine embroidery. As he finished his food and began to observe the details of the tapestry, the scenes thereon began to swim before his eyes. He looked questioningly at the Margravine, but her face was expressionless. His head felt light and he had lost the use of his limbs.

He tried to form words, but they would not come.

He had been drugged.

The woman had poisoned his food.

Once again he had allowed himself to become a victim of the Mabden.

He rested his head on his arms and fell, unwillingly, into a deep sleep.

Corum dreamed again.

He saw Castle Erorn as he had left it when he had first ridden out. He saw his father's wise face speaking and strained to hear the words, but could not. He saw his mother at work, writing her latest treatise on mathematics. He saw his sisters dancing to his uncle's new music.

The atmosphere was joyful.

But now he realized that he could not understand their activities. They seemed strange and pointless to him. They were like children playing, unaware that a savage beast stalked them.

He tried to cry out—to warn them—but he had no voice.

He saw fires begin to spring up in rooms—saw Mabden warriors who had entered the unprotected gates without the inhabitants being in the least aware of their presence. Laughing among themselves, the Mabden put the silk hangings and the furnishings to the torch.

Now he saw his kinfolk again. They had become aware of the fires and were rushing to seek their source.

His father came into a room in which Glandyth-a-Krae stood, hurling books onto a pyre he had erected in the middle of the chamber. His father watched in astonishment as Glandyth burned the books. His father's lips moved and his eyes were questioning—almost polite surprise.

Glandyth turned and grinned at him, drawing his axe from his belt. He raised the axe…

Now Corum saw his mother. Two Mabden held her while another heaved himself up and down on her naked body.

Corum tried to enter the scene, but something stopped him.

He saw his sisters and his cousin suffering the same fate as his mother. Again his path to them was blocked by something invisible.

He struggled to get through, but now the Mabden were slitting the girls' throats. They quivered and died like slain fawns.

Corum began to weep.

He was still weeping, but he lay against a warm body and from somewhere in the distance came a soothing voice.

His head was being stroked and he was being rocked back and forth in a soft bed by a woman on whose breast he lay.

For a moment he tried to free himself, but she held him tight.

He began to weep again, freely this time, great groans racking his body, until he slept again. And now the sleep was free from dreams...

He awoke feeling anxious. He felt that he had slept for too long, that he must be up and doing something. He half raised himself in the bed and then sank down again into the pillows.

It slowly came to him that he was much refreshed. For the first time since he had set off on his quest, he felt full of energy and well-being. Even the darkness in his mind seemed to have retreated.

So the Margravine had drugged him, but now, it seemed, it had been a drug to make him sleep, to help him regain his strength.

But how many days had he slept?

He stirred again in the bed and felt the soft warmth of another beside him, on his blind side. He turned his head and there was Rhalina, her eyes closed, her sweet face at peace.

He recalled his dreaming. He recalled the comfort he had been given as all the misery in him poured forth.

Rhalina had comforted him. He reached out with his good hand to stroke the tumbled hair. He felt affection for her—an affection almost as strong as he had felt for his own family.

Reminded of his dead kin, he stopped stroking her hair and contemplated, instead, the puckered stump of his left hand. It was completely healed now, leaving a rounded end of white skin. He looked back at Rhalina. How could she bear to share her bed with such a cripple?

As he looked at her, she opened her eyes and smiled at him.

He thought he detected pity in that smile and was immediately resentful. He began to climb from the bed, but her hand on his shoulder stopped him.

"Stay with me, Corum, for I need your comforting now."

He paused, looked back at her suspiciously.

"Please, Corum. I believe that I love you."

He frowned. "Love? Between Vadhagh and Mabden? Love of that kind?" He shook his head. "Impossible. There could be no issue."

"No children, I know. But love gives birth to other things…"

"I do not understand you."

"I am sorry," she said. "I was selfish. I am taking advantage of you." She sat up in bed. "I have slept with no-one else since my husband went away. I am not…"

Corum studied her body. It moved him and yet it should not have done. It was unnatural for one species to feel such emotion for another…

He reached down and kissed her breast. She clasped his head. They sank, again, into the sheets, making gentle love, learning of one another as only those truly in love may.

After some hours, she said to him, "Corum, you are the last of your race. I will never see my people again, save for those retainers who are here. It is peaceful in this castle. There is little that would disturb that peace. Would you not consider staying here with me—at least for a few months?"

"I have sworn to avenge the deaths of my folk," he reminded her softly, and kissed her cheek.

"Such oaths are not true to your nature, Corum. You are one who would rather love than hate, I know."

"I cannot answer that," he replied, "for I will not consider my life fulfilled unless I destroy Glandyth-a-Krae. This wish is not so hate-begotten as you might think. I feel, perhaps, like one who sees a disease spreading through a forest. One hopes to cut out the diseased plants so that the others may grow straight and live. That is my feeling concerning Glandyth-a-Krae. He has formed the habit of killing. Now that he has killed all the Vadhagh, he will want to kill others. If he finds no more strangers, he will begin to kill those wretches who occupy the villages ruled by Lyr-a-Brode. Fate has given me the impetus I need to pursue this attitude of mine to its proper conclusion, Rhalina."

"But why go from here now? Sooner or later we will receive news concerning this Glandyth. When that moment arrives, then you can set forth to exact your vengeance."

He pursed his lips. "Perhaps you are right."

"And you must learn to do without your hand and your eye," she said. "That will take much practice, Corum."

"True."

"So stay here, with me."

"I will agree to this much, Rhalina. I will make no decision for a few more days."

And Corum made no decision for a month. After the horror of his encounters with the Mabden raiders, his brain needed time to heal and this was difficult with the constant reminder of his injuries every time he automatically tried to use his left hand or glimpsed his reflection.

When not with him, Rhalina spent much of her time in the castle's library, but Corum had no taste for reading. He would walk about the battlements of the castle or take a horse and ride over the causeway at low tide (though Rhalina was perturbed by this for fear that he would fall prey to one of the Pony Tribes which occasionally ranged the area) and ride for a while among the trees.

And though the darkness in his mind became less noticeable as the pleasant days passed, it still remained. And Corum would sometimes pause in the middle of some action or stop when he witnessed some scene that reminded him of his home, the Castle Erorn.

The Margravine's castle was called simply Moidel's Castle and was raised on an island called Moidel's Mount, after the name of the family that had occupied it for centuries. It was full of interesting things. There were cabinets of porcelain and ivory figurines, rooms filled with curiosities taken at different times from the sea, chambers in which arms and armour were displayed, paintings (crude by Corum's standards) depicting scenes from the history of Lywm-an-Esh, as well as scenes taken from the legends and folktales of that land, which was rich in them. Such strange imaginings were rare among the Vadhagh, who had been a rational people, and they fascinated Corum. He came to realize that many of the stories concerning magical lands and weird beasts were derived from some knowledge of the other planes. Obviously the other planes had been glimpsed and the legend-makers had speculated freely from the fragments of knowledge thus gained. It amused Corum to trace a wild folktale back to its rather more mundane source, particularly where these folktales concerned the Old Races—the Vadhagh and the Nhadragh—who were attributed with the most alarming range of supernatural powers. He was also, by this study, offered some insight concerning the attitudes of the Mabden of the east, who seemed to have lived in awe of the Old Races before they had discovered that they were mortal and could be slain easily. It seemed to Corum that the vicious genocide engaged upon by these Mabden was partly caused by their hatred of the Vadhagh for *not* being the great seers and sorcerers the Mabden had originally thought them to be.

But this line of thought brought back the memories and the sorrow and the hatred and Corum would become depressed, sometimes for days, and even Rhalina's love could not console him then.

But then one day he inspected a tapestry in a room he had not previously visited and it absorbed his attention as he looked at the pictures and studied the embroidered text.

This was a complete legend telling of the adventures of Mag-an-Mag, a popular folk hero. Mag-an-Mag had been returning from a magical land when his boat had been set upon by pirates. These pirates had cut off Mag-an-Mag's arms and legs and thrown him overboard, then they had cut off the head of his companion, Jhakor-Neelus, and tossed his body after that of his master, but kept the head, apparently to eat. Eventually Mag-an-Mag's limbless body had been washed up on the shore of a mysterious island and Jhakor-Neelus's headless body had arrived at a spot a little further up the beach. These bodies were found by the servants of a magician who, in return for Mag-an-Mag's services against his enemies, offered to put back his limbs and make him as good as new. Mag-an-Mag had accepted on condition that the sorcerer find Jhakor-Neelus a new head. The sorcerer had agreed and furnished Jhakor-Neelus with the head of a crane, which seemed to please everyone. The pair then went on to fight the sorcerer's enemies and leave the island loaded down with his gifts.

Corum could find no origin for this legend in the knowledge of his own folk. It did not seem to fit with the others.

At first he dismissed his obsession with the legend as being fired by his own wish to get back the hand and the eye he had lost, but he remained obsessed.

Feeling embarrassed by his own interest, he said nothing of the legend to Rhalina for several weeks.

Autumn came to Moidel's Castle and with it a warm wind that stripped the trees bare and lashed the sea against the rocks and drove many of the birds away to seek a more restful clime.

And Corum began to spend more and more time in the room where hung the tapestry concerning Mag-an-Mag and the wonderful sorcerer. Corum began to realize that it was the text that chiefly interested him. It seemed to speak with an authority that was elsewhere lacking in the others he had seen.

But he still could not bring himself to tax Rhalina with questions concerning it.

Then, on one of the first days of winter, she sought for him and found him in the room and she did not seem surprised. However, she did show a certain concern, as if she had feared that he would find the tapestry sooner or later.

"You seem absorbed by the amusing adventures of Mag-an-Mag," she said. "They are only tales. Something to entertain us."

"But this one seems different," Corum said.

He turned to look at her. She was biting her lip.

"So it is different, Rhalina," Corum murmured. "You do know something about it!"

She began to shake her head, then changed her mind. "I know only what the old tales say. And the old tales are lies, are they not? Pleasing lies."

"Truth is somewhere in this tale, I feel. You must tell me what you know, Rhalina."

"I know more than is on this tapestry," she said quietly. "I have been lately reading a book that relates to it. I knew I had seen the book some years ago and I sought it out. I find quite recent reports concerning an island of the kind described. And there is, according to this book, an old castle there. The last person to see that island was an emissary of the Duchy, sailing here with supplies and greetings. And that was the last emissary to visit us…"

"How long ago? How long ago?"

"Thirty years."

And then Rhalina began to weep and shake her head and cough and try to control her tears.

He embraced her.

"Why do you weep, Rhalina?"

"I weep, Corum, because this means you will leave me. You will go away from Moidel's Castle in the wintertime and you will seek that island and perhaps you, too, will be wrecked. I weep because nothing I love stays with me."

Corum took a step back. "Has this thought been long in your mind?"

"It has been long in my mind."

"And you have not spoken it."

"Because I love you so much, Corum."

"You should not love me, Rhalina. And I should not have allowed myself to love you. Though this island offers me the faintest of hopes, I must seek it out."

"I know."

"And if I find the sorcerer and he gives me back my hand and eye—"

"Madness, Corum! He cannot exist!"

"But if he does and if he can do what I ask, then I will go to find Glandyth-a-Krae and I will kill him. Then, if I live, I will return. But Glandyth must die before I can know complete peace of mind, Rhalina."

She said softly, "There is no boat that is seaworthy."

"But there are boats in the harbour caves that can be made seaworthy."

"It will take several months to make one so."

"Will you lend me your servants to work on the boat?"

"Yes."

"Then I will speak to them at once."

And Corum left her, hardening his heart to the sight of her grief, blaming himself for letting himself fall in love with the woman.

With all the men he could muster who had some knowledge of shipcraft, Corum descended the steps that led from below the castle floor down through the rock to the sea-caves where the ships lay. He found one skiff that was in better repair than the others and he had it hauled upright and inspected.

Rhalina had been right. There was a great deal of work to be done before the skiff would safely ride the waters.

He would wait impatiently, though now that he had a

goal—no matter how wild—he began to feel a lessening of the weight that had been upon him.

He knew that he would never tire of loving Rhalina, but that he could never love her completely until his self-appointed task had been accomplished.

He rushed back to the library to consult the book she had mentioned. He found it and discovered that the name of the island was Svi-an-Fanla-Brool.

Svi-an-Fanla-Brool. Not a pleasant name. As far as Corum could make out it meant Home of the Gorged God. What could that mean? He inspected the text for an answer, but found none.

The hours passed as he copied out the charts and reference points given by the captain of the ship that had visited Moidel's Mount thirty years before. And it was very late when he sought his bed and found Rhalina there.

He looked down at her face. She had plainly wept herself to sleep.

He knew that it was his turn to offer her comfort.

But he had no time…

He undressed. He eased himself into the bed, between the silks and the furs, trying not to disturb her. But she stirred.

"Corum?"

He did not reply.

He felt her body tremble for a moment, but she did not speak again.

He sat up in bed, his mind full of conflict. He loved her. He should not love her. He tried to settle back, to go to sleep, but he could not.

He reached out and stroked her shoulder.

"Rhalina?"

"Yes, Corum?"

He took a deep breath, meaning to explain to her how strongly he needed to see Glandyth dead, to repeat that he would return when his vengeance was taken.

Instead he said, "Storms blow strongly now around Moidel's Castle. I will set aside my plans until the spring. I will stay until the spring."

She turned in the bed and peered through the darkness at his face. "You must do as you desire. Pity destroys true love, Corum."

"It is not pity that moves me."

"It is your sense of justice? That, too, is…"

"I tell myself that it is my sense of justice that makes me stay, but I know otherwise."

"Then why would you stay?"

"My resolve to go has weakened."

"What has weakened it, Corum?"

"Something quieter in me, yet something, perhaps, that is stronger. It is my love for you, Rhalina, that has conquered my desire to have immediate revenge on Glandyth. It is love. That is all I can tell you."

And she began to weep again, but it was not from sorrow.

A THOUSAND SWORDS

WINTER REACHED ITS fiercest. The towers seemed to shake with the force of the gales that raged around them. The seas smashed against the rocks of Moidel's Mount and sometimes the waves seemed to rise higher than the castle itself.

Days became almost as dark as night. Huge fires were lit in the castle, but they could not keep out the chill that was everywhere. Wool and leather and fur had to be worn at all times and the inhabitants of the castle lumbered about like bears in their thick garments.

Yet Corum and Rhalina, a man and a woman of alien species, hardly noticed the winter's brawling. They sang songs to each other and wrote simple sonnets concerning the depth and passion of their love. It was a madness that was upon them (if madness is that which denies certain fundamental realities) but it was a pleasant madness, a sweet madness.

Yet madness it was.

When the worst of the winter had gone, but before spring elected to show herself, when there was still snow on the rocks below the castle and few birds sang in the grey skies above the bare and distant forests of the mainland; when the sea had exhausted itself and now washed sullen and dark around the cliffs, that was when the strange Mabden were seen riding out of the black trees in the late morning, their breath steaming and their horses stumbling on the icy ground, their harness and their arms rattling.

It was Beldan who saw them first as he went onto the battlements to stretch his legs.

Beldan, the youth who had rescued Corum from the sea, turned and went hastily back into the tower and began to run down the steps until a figure blocked his way, laughing at him.

"The privy is above, Beldan, not below!"

Beldan drew a breath and spoke slowly. "I was on the way to your apartments, Prince Corum. I have seen them from the battlements. There is a large force."

Corum's face clouded and he seemed to be thinking a dozen thoughts at once. "Do you recognize the force? Who are they? Mabden?"

"Mabden, without doubt. I think they might be warriors of the Pony Tribes."

"The folk against whom this Margravate was built?"

"Aye. But they have not bothered us for a hundred years."

Corum smiled grimly. "Perhaps we all, in time, succumb to the ignorance that killed the Vadhagh. Can we defend the castle, Beldan?"

"If it is a small force, Prince Corum. The Pony Tribes are normally disunited and their warriors rarely move in bands of more than twenty or thirty."

"And do you think it is a small force?"

Beldan shook his head. "No, Prince Corum, I fear it is a large one."

"You had best alert the warriors. What about the bat creatures?"

"They sleep in winter. Nothing will wake them."

"What are your normal methods of defense?"

Beldan bit his lip.

"Well?"

"We have none to speak of. It has been so long since we needed to consider such things. The Pony Tribes still fear the power of Lywm-an-Esh—their fear is even superstitious since the land retreated beyond the horizon. We relied on that fear."

"Then do your best, Beldan, and I'll join you shortly, when I've taken a look at these warriors first. They may not come in war, for all we know."

Beldan raced away down the steps and Corum climbed the tower and opened the door and went out onto the battlements.

He saw that the tide was beginning to go out and that when it did the natural causeway between the mainland and the castle would be exposed. The sea was grey and chill, the shore was bleak. And the warriors were there.

They were shaggy men on shaggy ponies and they had helmets of iron with visors of brass beaten into the form of savage and evil faces. They had cloaks of wolfskin or wool, byrnies of iron, jackets of leather, trews of blue, red or yellow cloth bound around the feet and up to the knees with thongs. They were armed with spears, bows, axes, clubs. And each man had a sword strapped to the saddle of his pony. They were all new swords, Corum judged, for they glinted as if freshly forged, even in the dull light of that winter's day.

There were several ranks of them already on the beach and more were trotting from the forest.

Corum drew his sheepskin coat about him with his good hand and he kicked thoughtfully at one of the battlement stones, as if to reassure himself that the castle was solid.

He looked at the warriors on the beach again.

He counted a thousand.

A thousand riders with a thousand new-forged swords.

He frowned.

A thousand helmets of iron were turned towards Moidel's Castle. A thousand brass masks glared at Corum across the water as the tide slowly receded and the causeway began to appear below the surface.

Corum shivered. A gannet flew low over the silent throng and it shrieked as if in startled terror and climbed high into the clouds.

A deep drum began to sound from the forest. The metallic note was measured and slow and it echoed across the water.

It seemed that the thousand riders did not come in peace.

Beldan came out and joined Corum.

Beldan looked pale. "I have spoken to the Margravine and I have alerted our warriors. We have a hundred and fifty able men. The Margravine is consulting her husband's notes. He wrote a treatise on the best way to defend the castle in case of an attack of this kind. He knew that the Pony Tribes would unite one day, it seems."

"I wish I had read that treatise," said Corum. He swallowed a deep breath of the freezing air. "Is there none here with actual experience of war?"

"None, prince."

"Then we must learn rapidly."

"Aye."

There was a noise on the steps within the tower and brightly armoured men came out. Each was armed with a bow and many arrows. Each had a helmet on his head that was made from the curly-spined pink shell of a giant murex. Each controlled his fear.

"We will try to parley with them," murmured Corum, "when the causeway is clear. We will attempt to continue the conversation until the tide comes in again. This will give us a few more hours in which to prepare ourselves."

"They will suspect such a ruse, surely," Beldan said.

Corum nodded and rubbed at his cheek with his stump. "True. But if we—if we *lie* to them, regarding our strength, perhaps we shall be able to disconcert them a little."

Beldan gave a wry smile, but he said nothing. His eyes began to shine with an odd light. Corum thought he recognized it as battle-fever.

"I'll see what the Margravine has learned from her husband's texts," Corum said. "Stay here and watch, Beldan. Let me know if they begin to move."

"That damned drum!" Beldan pressed his hand to his temple. "It makes my brains shiver."

"Try to ignore it. It is meant to weaken our resolve."

Corum entered the tower and ran down the steps until he came to the floor where he and Rhalina had their apartments.

She was seated at a table with manuscripts spread out before her. She looked up as he entered and she tried to smile. "We are paying a price for the gift of love, it seems."

He looked at her in surprise. "That's a Mabden conception, I think. I do not understand it…"

"And I am a fool to make so shallow a statement. But I wish they had not chosen this time to come against us. They have had a hundred years to choose from…"

"What have you learned from your husband's notes?"

"Where our weakest positions are. Where our ramparts are best defended. I have already stationed men there. Cauldrons of lead are being heated."

"For what purpose?"

"You really do know little of war!" she said. "Less than do I. The molten lead will be poured on the heads of the invaders when they try to storm our walls."

Corum shuddered. "Must we be so crude?"

"We are not Vadhagh. We are not fighting Nhadragh. I believe you can expect these Mabden to have certain crude battle practices of their own…"

"Of course. I had best cast an eye over the Margrave's manuscripts. He was evidently a man who understood the realities."

"Aye," she said softly, handing him a sheet, "certain kinds of reality, at any rate."

It was the first time he had heard her offer an opinion of her husband. He stared at her, wanting to ask more, but she waved a delicate hand. "You had best read swiftly. You will understand the writing easily enough. My husband chose to write in the old High Speech we learned from the Vadhagh."

Corum looked at the writing. It was well-formed but without any individual character. It seemed to him that it was a somewhat soulless imitation of Vadhagh writing, but it was, as she had said, easy enough to understand.

There was a knock on the main door to their apartments. While Corum read, Rhalina went to answer it. A soldier stood there.

"Beldan sent me, Lady Margravine. He asked Prince Corum to join him on the battlements."

Corum put down the sheets of manuscript. "I will come immediately. Rhalina, will you see that my arms and armour are prepared?"

She nodded. He left.

The causeway was almost clear of water now. Beldan was yelling something across to the warriors on the bank, speaking of a parley.

The drum continued its slow but steady beat.

The warriors did not reply.

Beldan turned to Corum. "They might be dead men for all they'll respond. They seem singularly well-ordered for barbarians. I think there is some extra element to this situation that has not revealed itself as yet."

Corum had the same feeling. "Why did you send for me, Beldan?"

"I saw something in the trees. A flash of gold. I am not sure. Vadhagh eyes are said to be sharper than Mabden eyes. Tell me, prince, if you can make anything out. Over there." He pointed.

Corum's smile was bitter. "Two Mabden eyes are better than one Vadhagh..." But nonetheless he peered in the direction Beldan indicated. Sure enough there was something hidden by the trees. He altered the angle of his vision to see if he could make it out more clearly.

And then he realized what it was. It was a gold-decorated chariot wheel.

As he watched, the wheel began to turn. Horses emerged from the forest. Four shaggy horses, slightly larger than those ridden by the Pony Tribes, drawing a huge chariot in which stood a tall warrior.

Corum recognized the driver of the chariot. The Mabden was dressed in fur and leather and iron and had a winged helmet and a great beard and held himself proudly.

"It is Earl Glandyth-a-Krae, my enemy," said Corum softly.

Beldan said, "Is that the one who took off your hand and put out your eye?"

Corum nodded.

"Then perhaps it is he who has united the Pony Tribes and given them those bright new swords they carry, and drilled them to the order they now hold."

"I think it likely. I have brought this upon Moidel's Castle, Beldan."

Beldan shrugged. "It would have come. You made our Margravine happy. I have never known her happy, before, prince."

"You Mabden seem to think that happiness must be bought with misery."

"I suppose we do."

"It is not easy for a Vadhagh to understand that. We believe—believed—that happiness was a natural condition of reasoning beings."

Now from the forest emerged another twenty chariots. They arranged themselves behind Glandyth so that the Earl of Krae was between the silent, masked warriors and his own followers, the Denledhyssi.

The drum stopped its beating.

Corum listened to the tide drawing back. Now the causeway was completely exposed.

"He must have followed me, learned where I was and spent the winter recruiting and training those warriors," Corum said.

"But how did he discover your hiding place?" Beldan said.

For answer, the ranks of the Pony Tribes opened and Glandyth drove his chariot down towards the causeway. He bent and picked something from the floor of his chariot, raised it above his head and flung it over the backs of his horses to fall upon the causeway.

Corum shuddered when he recognized it.

Beldan stiffened and stretched out his hand to grasp the stone of the battlement, lowering his head.

"Is it the Brown Man, Prince Corum?"

"It is."

"The creature was so innocent. So kind. Could not its master save it? They must have tortured it to get the information concerning your whereabouts…"

Corum straightened his back. His voice was soft and cold when he spoke next. "I once told your mistress that Glandyth was a disease that must be stopped. I should have sought him out sooner, Beldan."

"He would have killed you."

"But he would not have killed the Brown Man of Laahr. Serwde would still be serving his sad master. I think there is a doom upon me, Beldan. I think I am meant to be dead and that all those who help me to continue living are doomed also. I will go out now and fight Glandyth alone. Then the castle will be saved."

Beldan swallowed and spoke hoarsely. "We chose to help you. You did not ask for that help. Let us choose when we shall take back that help."

"No. For if you do, the Margravine and all her people will surely perish."

"They will perish anyway," Beldan told him.

"Not if I let Glandyth take me."

"Glandyth must have offered the Pony Tribes this castle as a prize if they would assist him," Beldan pointed out. "They do not care about you. They wish to destroy and loot something that they have hated for centuries. Certainly it is likely that Glandyth would be content with you—he would go away—but he would leave his thousand swords behind. We must all fight together, Prince Corum. There is nothing else for it now."

THE SUMMONING

CORUM RETURNED TO his apartments where his arms and his armour had been laid out for him. The armour was unfamiliar, consisting of breastplate, backplate, greaves and a kilt all made from the pearly blue shells of a sea creature called the *anufec*, which had once inhabited the waters of the west. The shell was stronger than the toughest iron and lighter than any byrnie. A great, spined helmet with a jutting peak had, like the helmets of the other warriors of Moidel's Castle, been manufactured from the shell of the giant murex. Servants helped Corum don his gear and they gave him a huge iron broadsword that was so well balanced that he could hold it in his one good hand. His shield, which he had them strap to his handless arm, was the shell of a massive crab which had once lived, the servants told him, in a place far beyond even Lywm-an-Esh and known as the Land of the Distant Sea. This armour had belonged to the dead Margrave who had inherited it from his ancestors who had owned it long before it had been considered necessary to establish a Margravate at all.

Corum called to Rhalina as he was prepared for battle, but
although he could see her through the doors dividing the
chambers, she did not look up from her papers. It was the last
of the Margrave's manuscripts and it seemed to absorb her more
than the others.

Corum left to return to the battlements.

Save for the fact that Glandyth's chariot was now on the
approach to the causeway, the ranks of the warriors had not
shifted. The little broken corpse of the Brown Man of Laahr still
lay on the causeway.

The drum had begun to beat again.

"Why do they not advance?" Beldan said, his voice sharp with
tension.

"Perhaps for a twofold reason," Corum replied. "They are
hoping to terrify us and banish the terror in themselves."

"They are terrified of us?"

"The Pony Tribesmen probably are. After all, they have, as
you told me yourself, lived in superstitious fear of the folk of
Lywm-an-Esh for centuries. They doubtless suspect we have
supernatural means of defense."

Beldan could not restrain an ironic grin. "You begin to
understand the Mabden at last, Prince Corum. Better than I,
it seems."

Corum gestured towards Glandyth-a-Krae. "There is the
Mabden who gave me my first lesson."

"He seems without fear, at least."

"He does not fear swords, but he fears himself. Of all Mabden traits, I would say that that was the most destructive."

Now Glandyth was raising a gauntleted hand.

Again silence fell.

"Vadhagh!" came the savage voice. "Can you see who it is who has come to call on you in the castle of vermin?"

Corum did not reply. Hidden by a battlement, he watched as Glandyth scanned the ramparts, seeking him out.

"Vadhagh! Are you there?"

Beldan looked questioningly at Corum who continued to remain silent.

"Vadhagh! You see we have destroyed your demon familiar! Now we are going to destroy you—and those most despicable of Mabden who have given you shelter. Vadhagh! Speak!"

Corum murmured to Beldan. "We must stretch this pause as far as it will go. Every second brings the tide back to cover our causeway."

"They will strike soon," Beldan said. "Well before the tide returns."

"Vadhagh! Oh, you are the most cowardly of a cowardly race!"

Corum now saw Glandyth begin to turn his head back towards his men, as if to give the order to attack. He emerged from his cover and raised his voice.

His speech, even in cold anger, was liquid music compared with Glandyth's rasping tones.

"Here I am, Glandyth-a-Krae, most wretched and pitiable of Mabden!"

Disconcerted, Glandyth turned his head back. Then he burst into raucous laughter. "I am not the wretch!" He reached inside his furs and drew something out that was on a string round his neck. "Would you come and fetch this back from me?"

Corum felt bile come when he saw what Glandyth sported. It

was Corum's own mummified hand, still bearing the ring that his sister had given him.

"And look!" Glandyth took a small leather bag from his furs and waved it at Corum. "I have also saved your eye!"

Corum controlled his hatred and his nausea and called, "You may have the rest, Glandyth, if you will turn back your horde and depart from Moidel's Castle in peace."

Glandyth flung his chin towards the sky and roared with laughter. "Oh, no, Vadhagh! They would not let me rob them of a fight—let alone their prize. They have waited many months for this. They are going to slay all their ancient enemies. And I am going to slay you. I had planned to spend the winter in the comfort of Lyr-a-Brode's Court. Instead I have had to camp in skin tents with our friends here. I intend to slay you quickly, Vadhagh, I promise you. I have no more time to spend on a crippled piece of offal, such as yourself." He laughed again. "Who is the 'half-thing' now?"

"Then you would not be afraid to fight me alone," Corum called. "You could do battle on this causeway with me and doubtless kill me very quickly. Then you could leave the castle to your friends and return to your own land the faster."

Glandyth frowned, debating this with himself.

"Why should you sacrifice your life a little earlier than you need to?"

"I am tired of living as a cripple. I am tired of fearing you and your men."

Glandyth was not convinced. Corum was trying to buy time with his talk and his suggestion, but on the other hand it did not matter to Glandyth how much trouble the Pony Tribesmen would be forced to go, to take the castle after he had killed Corum.

Eventually he nodded, shouting back, "Very well, Vadhagh,

come down to the causeway. I will tell my men to stand off until we have had our fight. If you kill me, I will have my charioteers leave the battle to the others…"

"I do not believe that part of your bargain," Corum replied. "I am not interested in it, either. I will come down."

Corum took his time descending the steps. He did not want to die at Glandyth's hand and he knew that if Glandyth did, by some luck, fall to him, the Earl of Krae's men would swiftly leap to their master's assistance. All he hoped for was to gain a few hours for the defenders.

Rhalina met him outside their apartments.

"Where go you, Corum?"

"I go to fight Glandyth and most probably to die," he said. "I shall die loving you, Rhalina."

Her face was a mask of horror. "Corum! No!"

"It is necessary, if this castle is to have a chance of withstanding those warriors."

"No, Corum! There may be a way to get help. My husband speaks of it in his treatise. A last resort."

"What help?"

"He is vague on that score. It is something passed on to him by his forefathers. A Summoning. Sorcery, Corum."

Corum smiled sadly. "There is no such thing as sorcery, Rhalina. What you call sorcery is a handful of half-learned scraps of Vadhagh wisdom."

"This is not Vadhagh wisdom—it is something else. A Summoning."

He made to move past her. She held his arm. "Corum, let me try the Summoning!"

He pulled his arm away and, sword in hand, continued down the steps. "Very well, try what you will, Rhalina. Even if you are right, you will need the time I can gain for you."

He heard her shout wordlessly and he heard her sob, and then he had reached the hall and was walking towards the great main gates of the castle.

A startled warrior let him through and he stood at last upon the causeway. At the other end, his chariot and horses led away, the body of the Brown Man kicked to one side, stood Earl Glandyth-a-Krae. And beside Glandyth-a-Krae, holding his war-axe for him, was the gawky figure of the youth, Rodlik.

Glandyth reached out and tousled his page's hair and bared his teeth in a wolfish grin. He took the axe from the youth's hand and began to advance along the causeway.

Corum walked to meet him.

The sea slapped against the rocks of the causeway. Sometimes a seabird cried out. There was no sound from the warriors of either side. Both defenders and attackers watched tensely as the two approached each other and then, in the middle, stopped. About ten feet separated them.

Corum saw that Glandyth had grown a little thinner. But the pale, grey eyes still contained that strange, unnatural glint and the face was just as red and unhealthy as the last time Corum had seen it. He held his war-axe down in front of him, in his two hands, his helmeted head on one side.

"By the Dog," he said, "you have become hugely ugly, Vadhagh."

"We make a fine pair, then, Mabden, for you have changed not at all."

Glandyth sneered. "And you are hung all about with pretty shells, I see, like some sea god's daughter going to be wed to her fishy husband. Well, you may become their nuptial feast when I throw your body into the sea."

Corum wearied of these heavy insults. He leapt forward

and swung his great broadsword at Glandyth who brought his metal-shod axe haft up swiftly and blocked the blow, staggering a little. He kept his axe in his right hand and drew his long knife, dropped to a crouch and aimed the axe at Corum's knees.

Corum jumped high and the axe blade whistled under his feet. He stabbed out at Glandyth and the blade scraped the Mabden's shoulder plate but did not harm him.

Nonetheless Glandyth cursed and tried the same trick again. Again Corum jumped and the axe missed him. Glandyth sprang back and brought the axe down on the crabshell shield which creaked with the strain of the blow, but did not shatter, though Corum's arm was numb from wrist to shoulder. He retaliated with an overarm blow which Glandyth blocked.

Corum kicked out at Glandyth's legs, hoping to knock him off balance, but the Mabden ran backwards several paces before standing his ground again.

Corum advanced cautiously towards him.

Then Glandyth cried out, "I'm tired of this. We have him now. Archers—shoot!"

And then Corum saw the charioteers who had moved quietly down to the forefront of the ranks and were aiming their bows at him. He raised his shield to protect himself against their arrows.

Glandyth was running back down the causeway.

Corum had been betrayed. There was still an hour before the tide came in. It seemed he was going to die for nothing.

Now another shout, this time from the castle's battlements, and a wave of arrows swept down. Beldan's archers had shot first.

The Denledhyssi arrows rattled on Corum's shield and against his greaves. He felt something bite into his leg just above the knee, where he had scant protection. He looked down. It was an arrow. It had passed completely through his leg and now half of it stuck out behind his knee. He tried to stumble backwards, but it was hard to run with the arrow in him. To pull it out with his only hand would mean he would have to drop his sword. He glanced towards the shore.

As he had known they would, the first of the horsemen were beginning to cross.

He began to drag himself back along the causeway for a few more yards and then he knew he would never reach the gates in time. Quickly he knelt on his good leg, put his sword on the ground, snapped off part of the arrow at the front and drew the rest through his leg, flinging it to one side.

He picked up his sword again and prepared to stand his ground.

The warriors in the brass war-masks were galloping along the causeway two abreast, their new swords in their hands.

Corum struck at the first rider and his blow was a lucky one, for it hurled the man from his saddle. The other rider had tried to strike at Corum but had missed and overshot.

Corum swung himself up into the pony's primitive saddle. For stirrups there were just two leather loops hanging from the girth strap. Painfully, Corum managed to get his feet into these and block the sword blow from the returning rider. Another rider came up now and his sword clanged on Corum's shield. The horses were snorting and trying to rear, but the causeway was so narrow there was little room for manoeuvre and neither Corum nor the other two could use their swords effectively as they tried to control their half-panicked horses.

The rest of the masked riders were forced to rein in their beasts for fear of toppling off the causeway into the sea and this gave Beldan's archers the opportunity they required. Dark sheets of arrows sped from the battlements and into the ranks of the Pony Tribesmen. More ponies went down than men, but it added further to the confusion.

Slowly Corum retreated down the causeway until he was almost at the gate. His shield arm was completely paralyzed and his sword-arm aching dreadfully, but he still managed to continue defending himself against the riders.

Glandyth was screaming at the pony barbarians, trying to force them to retreat and regroup. Evidently his plans of attack had not been followed. Corum managed to grin. At least that was something he had gained.

Now the gates of the castle suddenly opened behind him. Beldan stood there with fifty archers poised to shoot.

"In, Corum, quickly!" Beldan cried.

Understanding Beldan's intention, Corum flung himself from the back of the pony and bent double, running towards the gates as the first flight of arrows rushed over his head. Then he was through the gates and they had closed.

Corum leaned panting against a pillar. He felt he had failed in his intention. But now Beldan was slapping his shoulder.

"The tide's coming in, Corum! We succeeded!"

The slap was enough to topple Corum. He saw Beldan's surprised expression as he fell to the flagstones and for a moment he was amused by the situation before he passed out completely.

As he awoke, in his own bed with Rhalina sitting at the table nearby, still reading from the manuscripts, Corum realized that no matter how well he trained himself to fight, no matter how well he had survived during the battle of the causeway, he would not survive long in the Mabden world with both a hand and an eye gone.

"I must have a new hand," he said, sitting upright. "I must have a new eye, Rhalina."

Rhalina did not appear to hear him at first. Then she looked up. Her face was tired and drawn in lines of heavy concentration. Absently, she said, "Rest," and returned to her reading.

There was a knock. Beldan came in quickly. Corum began to get out of bed. He winced as he moved. His wounded leg was stiff and his whole body was bruised.

"They lost some thirty men in that encounter," Beldan said. "The tide goes out again just before sunset. I'm not sure if they'll try another attack then. I would say they will wait until morning."

Corum frowned. "It depends on Glandyth, I'd say. He would judge that we wouldn't expect an evening attack and would therefore try to make one. But if those Pony Tribesmen are as superstitious as we think, they might be reluctant to fight at night. We had best prepare for an attack on the next tide. And guard all sides of the castle. How does that match with the Margrave's treatise, Rhalina?"

She looked up vaguely, nodding. "Well enough."

Corum began painfully to buckle on his armour. Beldan helped him. They left for the battlements.

The Denledhyssi had regrouped on the shore. The dead men and their ponies, as well as the corpse of the Brown Man of Laahr, had been washed away by the sea. A few corpses bobbed among the rocks below the castle.

They had formed the same ranks as earlier. The mounted masked riders were massed some ten ranks deep with Glandyth behind them and the charioteers behind Glandyth.

Cauldrons of lead bubbled on fires built on the battlements; small catapults had been erected, with piles of stone balls beside them, for ammunition; extra arrows and javelins were heaped by the far wall.

Again the tide was retreating.

The metallic drum began to beat again. There was the distant jingle of harness. Glandyth was speaking to some of the horsemen.

"I think he will attack," said Corum.

The sun was low and all the world seemed turned to a dark, chill grey. They watched as the causeway gradually became exposed until only a foot or two of water covered it.

Then the beat of the drum became more rapid. There was a howl from the riders. They began to move forward and splash onto the causeway.

The real battle for Moidel's Castle had begun.

Not all the horsemen rode along the causeway. About two thirds of the force remained on the shore. Corum guessed what this meant.

"Are all points of the castle guarded now, Beldan?"

"They are, Prince Corum."

"Good. I think they'll try to swim their horses round and get a hold on the rocks so that they can attack from all sides. When darkness falls, have flare arrows shot regularly at all quarters."

Then the horsemen were storming the castle. The cauldrons of lead were upended and beasts and riders screamed in pain as the white-hot metal flooded over them. The sea hissed and steamed as the lead hit it. Some of the riders had brought up battering rams, slung between their mounts. They began to charge at the gates. Riders were shot from their saddles, but the horses ran wildly on. One of the rams struck the gates and smashed into them and through them, becoming jammed. The riders strove to extricate it, but could not. They were struck by a wave of boiling lead, but the ram remained.

"Get archers to the gates," Corum commanded. "And have horses ready in case the main hall is breached."

It was almost dark, but the fight continued. Some of the barbarians were riding round the lower parts of the hill. Corum saw the next rank leave the shore and begin to swim their horses through the shallow waters.

But Glandyth and his charioteers remained on the beach taking no part in the battle. Doubtless Glandyth planned to wait until the castle defenses were breached before he crossed the causeway.

Corum's hatred of the Earl of Krae had increased since the betrayal earlier that day and now he saw him using the superstitious barbarians for his own purposes, Corum knew that his judgment of Glandyth was right. The man would corrupt anything with which he came in contact.

All around the castle now, the defenders were dying from spear and arrow wounds. At least fifty were dead or badly hurt and the remaining hundred were spread very thinly.

Corum made a rapid tour of the defenses, encouraging the warriors to greater efforts, but now the boiling lead was finished and arrows and spears were running short. Soon the hand-to-hand fighting would begin.

Night fell. Flare arrows revealed bands of barbarians all around the castle. Beacons burned on the battlements. The fighting continued.

The barbarians reconcentrated on the main gates. More rams were brought up. The gates began to groan and give way.

Corum took all the men he could spare into the main hall.

There they mounted their horses and formed a semicircle behind the archers, waiting for the barbarians to come through.

More rams pierced the gates and Corum heard the sound of swords and axes beating on the splintered timbers outside.

Suddenly they were through, yelling and howling. Firelight glinted on their masks of brass, making them look even more evil and terrifying. Their ponies snorted and reared.

There was time for only one wave of arrows, then the archers retreated to make way for Corum and his cavalry to charge the disconcerted barbarians.

Corum's sword smashed into a mask, sheared through it and destroyed the face beneath. Blood splashed high and a nearby brand fizzed as the liquid hit it.

Forgetful of the pain of his wounds, Corum swung the sword back and forth, knocking riders from their mounts, striking heads from shoulders, limbs from bodies. But slowly he and his remaining men were retreating as fresh waves of Pony Tribesmen surged into the castle.

Now they were at the far end of the hall, where a stone stairway curled up to the next floor. The archers were positioned here, along the stairs, and began to shoot their arrows into the barbarians. The barbarians not directly engaged with Corum's men retaliated with javelins and arrows and slowly Moidel's archers fell.

Corum glanced around him as he fought. There were few left with him—perhaps a dozen—and there were some fifty barbarians in the hall. The fight was nearing its conclusion. Within moments he and his friends would all be dead.

He saw Beldan begin to descend the stairs. At first Corum thought he was bringing up reinforcements, but he had only two warriors with him.

"Corum! Corum!"

Corum was pressed by two barbarians. He could not reply.

"Corum! Where is the Lady Rhalina?"

Corum found extra strength now. He delivered a blow to the first barbarian's skull which killed him. He kicked the man from his saddle, then stood on the back of his horse and jumped to the stairs. "What? Is the Lady Rhalina in danger?"

"I do not know, prince. I cannot discover where she is. I fear…"

Corum raced up the stairs.

From below the noise of the battle was changing. There seemed to be disconcerted shouts coming from the barbarians. He paused and looked back.

The barbarians were beginning to retreat in panic.

Corum could not understand what was happening, but he had no more time to watch.

He reached his apartments. "Rhalina! Rhalina!"

No reply.

Here and there were the bodies of their own warriors and barbarians who had managed to sneak into the castle through poorly defended windows and balconies.

Had Rhalina been taken by a party of barbarians?

Then, from the balcony of her apartment, he heard a strange sound.

It was a singing sound, like nothing he had experienced before. He paused, then approached the balcony cautiously.

Rhalina stood there and she was singing. The wind caught her garments and spread them about her like strange, multicoloured clouds. Her eyes were fixed on the far distance and her throat vibrated with the sounds she made.

She seemed to be in a trance and Corum made no sound, but watched. The words she sang were in no language he knew.

Doubtless it was an ancient Mabden language. It made him shudder.

Then she stopped and turned in his direction. But she did not see him. Still in the trance, she walked straight past him and back into the room.

Corum peered around a buttress. He had seen an odd green light shining in the direction of the mainland.

He saw nothing more, but heard the yells of the barbarians as they splashed about near the causeway. There was no doubt now but they were retreating.

Corum entered the apartments. Rhalina was sitting in her chair by the table. She was stiff and could not hear him when he murmured her name. Hoping that she would succumb no further to the peculiar trance, he left the room and ran for the main battlements.

Beldan was already there, his jaw slack as he watched what was taking place.

There was a huge ship rounding the headland to the north. It was the source of the strange green light and it sailed rapidly, though there was no wind at all now. The barbarians were scrambling onto their horses, or plunging on foot through the water that was beginning to cover the causeway. They seemed mad with fear. From the darkness on the shore, Corum heard Glandyth cursing them and trying to make them go back.

The ship flickered with many small fires, it seemed. Its masts and its hull seemed encrusted with dull jewels. And Corum saw what the barbarians had seen. He saw the crew. Flesh rotted on their faces and limbs.

The ship was crewed by corpses.

"What is it, Beldan?" he whispered. "Some artful illusion?"

Beldan's voice was hoarse. "I do not think it is an illusion, Prince Corum."

"Then what?"

"It is a Summoning. That is the old Margrave's ship. It has been drawn up to the surface. Its crew has been given something like life. And see—" he pointed to the figure on the poop deck, a skeletal creature in armour which, like Corum's, was made from great shells, whose sunken eyes flickered with the same green fire that covered the ship like weed—"there is the Margrave himself. Returned to save his castle."

Corum forced himself to watch as the apparition drew closer.

"And what else has he returned for, I wonder?" he said.

# 12

THE MARGRAVE'S BARGAIN

THE SHIP REACHED the causeway and stopped. It reeked of ozone and of decay.

"If it be an illusion," Corum murmured grimly, "it is a good one."

Beldan made no reply.

In the distance they heard the barbarians blundering off through the forest. They heard the sound of the chariots turning as Glandyth pursued his allies.

Though all the corpses were armed, they did not move, simply turned their heads, as one, towards the main gate of the castle.

Corum was transfixed in astonished terror. The events he was witnessing were like something from the superstitious mind of a Mabden. They could have no existence in actuality. Such images were those created by ignorant fear and morbid imagination. They were something from the crudest and most barbaric of the tapestries he had looked at in the castle.

"What will they do now, Beldan?"

"I have no understanding of the occult, prince. The Lady Rhalina is the only one of us who has made some study of such things. It was she who made this Summoning. I only know that there is said to be a bargain involved…"

"A bargain?"

Beldan gasped. "The Margravine!"

Corum saw that Rhalina, still walking in a trance, had left the gates and was moving, calf-deep, along the causeway towards the ship. The head of the dead Margrave turned slightly and the green fire in his eye-sockets seemed to burn more deeply.

"NO!"

Corum raced from the battlements, leapt down the stairway and stumbled through the main hall over the corpses of the fallen.

"NO! Rhalina! NO!"

He reached the causeway and began to wade after her, the stench from the ship of the dead choking him.

"Rhalina!"

It was a dream worse than any he had had since Glandyth's destruction of Castle Erorn.

"Rhalina!"

She had almost reached the ship when Corum caught up with her and seized her by the arm with his good hand.

She, seeming oblivious of him, continued to try to reach the ship.

"Rhalina! What bargain did you make to save us? Why did this ship of the dead come here?"

Her voice was cold, toneless. "I will join my husband now."

"No, Rhalina. Such a bargain cannot be honoured. It is obscene. It is evil. It—it…" He tried to express his knowledge that such things as this could not exist, that they were all under some peculiar hallucination. "Come back with me, Rhalina.

Let the ship return to the depths."

"I must go with it. Those were the terms of our bargain."

He clung to her, trying to drag her back, and then another voice spoke. It was a voice that seemed without substance and yet which echoed in his skull and made him pause.

"She sails with us, Prince of the Vadhagh. This must be."

Corum looked up. The dead Margrave had raised his hand in a commanding gesture. The eyes of fire burned deeply into Corum's single eye.

Corum tried to alter his perspective, to see into the other dimensions around him. At last he succeeded.

But it made no difference. The ship was in each of the five dimensions. He could not escape it.

"I will not let her sail with you," Corum replied. "Your bargain was unjust. Why should she die?"

"She does not die. She will awaken soon."

"What? Beneath the waves?"

"She has given this ship life. Without it, we shall sink again. With her on board, we live."

"Live? You do not live."

"It is better than death."

"Then death must be something more awful than I imagined."

"For us it is, Prince of the Vadhagh. We are the slaves of Shool-an-Jyvan, for we died in the waters he rules. Now, let us be rejoined, my wife and myself."

"No." Corum took a firmer grip on Rhalina's arm. "Who is this Shool-an-Jyvan?"

"He is our master. He is of Svi-an-Fanla-Brool."

"The Home of the Gorged God!" The place where Corum had meant to go before Rhalina's love had kept him at Moidel's Castle.

"Now. Let my wife come aboard."

"What can you do to make me? You are dead! You have only the power to frighten away barbarians."

"We saved your life. Now give us the means to live. She must come with us."

"The dead are selfish."

The corpse nodded and the green fire dimmed a little. "Aye. The dead are selfish."

Now Corum saw that the rest of the crew were beginning to move. He heard the slithering of their feet on the slime-grown deck. He saw their rotting flesh, their glowing eye-sockets. He began to move backwards, dragging Rhalina with him. But Rhalina would not go willingly and he was completely exhausted. Panting, he paused, speaking urgently to her. "Rhalina. I know you never loved him, even in life. You love me. I love you. Surely that is stronger than any bargain!"

"I must join my husband."

The dead crew had descended to the causeway and were moving towards them. Corum had left his sword behind. He had no weapons.

"Stand back!" he cried. "The dead have no right to take the living!"

On came the corpses.

Corum cried up to the figure of the Margrave, still on the poop deck. "Stop them! Take me instead of her! Make a bargain with me!"

"I cannot."

"Then let me sail with her. What is the harm in that? You will have two living beings to warm your dead souls!"

The Margrave appeared to consider this.

"Why should you do it? The living have no liking for the dead."

"I love Rhalina. It is love, do you understand?"

"Love? The dead know nothing of love."

"Yet you want your wife with you."

"She proposed the bargain. Shool-an-Jyvan heard her and sent us."

The shuffling corpses had completely surrounded them now. Corum gagged at their stench.

"Then I will come with you."

The dead Margrave inclined his head.

Escorted by the shuffling corpses, Corum allowed himself and Rhalina to be led aboard the ship. It was covered in scum from the bottom of the sea. Weed draped it, giving off the strange green fire. What Corum had thought were dull jewels were coloured barnacles which encrusted everything. Slime lay on all surfaces.

While the Margrave watched from his poop deck, Corum and Rhalina were taken to a cabin and made to enter. It was almost pitch-black and it stank of decay.

He heard the rotting timbers creak and the ship began to move.

It sailed rapidly, without wind or any other understandable means of propulsion.

It sailed for Svi-an-Fanla-Brool, the island of the legends, the Home of the Gorged God.

BOOK TWO

IN WHICH PRINCE CORUM RECEIVES
A GIFT AND MAKES A PACT

THE AMBITIOUS SORCERER

As they sailed through the night, Corum made many attempts to waken Rhalina from her trance, but nothing worked. She lay among the damp and rotting silks of a bunk and stared at the roof. Through a porthole too small to afford escape came a faint green light. Corum paced the cabin, still barely able to believe his predicament.

These were plainly the dead Margrave's own quarters. And if Corum were not here now, would the Margrave be sharing the bunk with his wife…?

Corum shuddered and pressed his hand to his skull, certain that he was insane or had been entranced—certain that none of this could be.

As a Vadhagh he was prepared for many events and situations that would have seemed strange to the Mabden. Yet this was something that seemed completely unnatural to him. It defied all he knew of science. If he were sane and all was as it seemed, then the Mabden's powers were greater than anything the Vadhagh had known. Yet they were dark and morbid powers, unhealthy powers that were quintessentially evil…

Corum was tired, but he could not sleep. Everything he touched was slimy and made him feel ill. He tested the lock on the cabin door. Although the wood was rotten, the door seemed unusually strong. Some other force was at work here. The timbers of the ship were bound by more than rivets and tar.

The weariness did not help his head to clear. His thoughts remained confused and desperate. He peered frequently through the porthole, hoping to get some sort of bearing, but it was impossible to see anything more than the occasional wave and a star in the sky.

Then, much later, he noticed the first line of grey on the horizon and he was relieved that morning was coming. This ship was a ship of the night. It would disappear with the sun and he and Rhalina would awake to find themselves in their own bed.

But what had frightened the barbarians? Or was that part of the dream? Perhaps his collapse within the gates after his fight with Glandyth had induced a feverish dream? Perhaps his comrades were still fighting for their lives against the Pony Tribesmen. He rubbed his head with the stump of his hand. He licked his dry lips and tried to peer, once again, into the dimensions. But the other dimensions were closed to him. He paced the cabin, waiting for the morning.

But then a strange droning sound came to his ears. It made his brain itch. He wrinkled his scalp. He rubbed his face. The droning increased. His ears ached. His teeth were on edge. The volume grew.

He put his good hand to one ear and covered the other with his arm. Tears came into his eye. In the socket where the other eye had been a huge pain pulsed.

He stumbled from side to side of the rotting cabin and even attempted to break through the door.

But his senses were leaving him. The scene grew dim…

…He stood in a dark hall with walls of fluted stone which curved over his head and touched to form the roof, high above. The workmanship of the hall was equal to anything the Vadhagh had created, but it was not beautiful. Rather, it was sinister.

His head ached.

The air before him shimmered with a pale blue light and then a tall youth stood there. The face was young, but the eyes were ancient. He was dressed in a simple flowing gown of yellow samite. He bowed, turned his back, walked a little way and then sat down on a stone bench that had been built into the wall.

Corum frowned.

"You believe you dream, Master Corum?"

"I am Prince Corum in the Scarlet Robe, last of the Vadhagh race."

"There are no other princes here, but me," said the youth softly. "I will allow none. If you understand that, there will be no tension between us."

Corum shrugged. "I believe I dream, yes."

"In a sense you do, of course. As we all dream. For some while, Vadhagh, you have been trapped in a Mabden dream. The rules of the Mabden control your fate and you resent it."

"Where is the ship that brought me here? Where is Rhalina?"

"The ship cannot sail by day. It has returned to the depths."

"Rhalina?"

The youth smiled. "She has gone with it, of course. That was the bargain she made."

"Then she is dead?"

"No. She lives."

"How can she live when she is below the surface of the ocean!"

"She lives. She always will. She cheers the crew enormously."

"Who are you?"

"I believe you have guessed my name."

"Shool-an-Jyvan."

"Prince Shool-an-Jyvan, Lord of All That Is Dead in the Sea—one of my several titles."

"Give me back Rhalina."

"I intend to."

Corum looked suspiciously at the sorcerer. "What?"

"You do not think I would bother to answer such a feeble attempt at a Summoning as the one she made, do you, if I did not have other motives in mind?"

"Your motive is clear. You relished the horror of her predicament."

"Nonsense. Am I so childish? I have outgrown such things. I see you are beginning to argue in Mabden terms. It is just as well for you, if you wish to survive in this Mabden dream."

"It is a dream…?"

"Of sorts. Real enough. It is what you might call the dream of a god. There again you might say that it is a dream that a god has allowed to become reality. I refer of course to the Knight of the Swords who rules the Five Planes."

"The Sword Rulers! They do not exist. It is a superstition once entertained by the Vadhagh and the Nhadragh."

"The Sword Rulers do exist, Master Corum. You have one of them, at least, to thank for your misfortunes. It was the Knight of the Swords who decided to let the Mabden grow strong and destroy the Old Races."

"Why?"

"Because he was bored by you. Who would not be? The world has become more interesting now, I'm sure you will agree."

"Chaos and destruction is 'interesting'?" Corum made an impatient gesture. "I thought you had outgrown such childish ideas."

Shool-an-Jyvan smiled. "Perhaps I have. But has the Knight of the Swords?"

"You do not speak plainly, Prince Shool."

"True. A vice I find impossible to give up. Still, it enlivens a dull conversation sometimes."

"If you are bored with this conversation, return Rhalina to me and I will leave."

Shool smiled again. "I have it in my power to bring Rhalina back to you and to set you free. That is why I let Master Moidel answer her Summoning. I wished to meet you, Master Corum."

"You did not know I would come."

"I thought it likely."

"Why did you wish to meet me?"

"I have something to offer you. In case you refused my gift, I thought it wise to have Mistress Rhalina on hand."

"And why should I refuse a gift?"

Shool shrugged. "My gifts are sometimes refused. Folk are suspicious of me. The nature of my calling disturbs them. Few have a kind word for a sorcerer, Master Corum."

Corum peered around him in the gloom. "Where is the door? I will seek Rhalina myself. I am very weary, Prince Shool."

"Of course you are. You have suffered much. You thought your own sweet dream a reality and you thought reality a dream. A shock. There is no door. I have no need of them. Will you not hear me out?"

"If you choose to speak in a less elliptical manner, aye."

"You are a poor guest, Vadhagh. I thought your race a courteous one."

"I am no longer typical."

"A shame that the last of a race should not typify its virtues. However, I am, I hope, a better host and I will comply with your request. I am an ancient being. I am not of the Mabden and I am not of the folk you call the Old Races. I came before you. I belonged to a race which began to degenerate. I did not wish to degenerate and so I concerned myself with the discovery of scientific ways in which I could preserve my mind in all its wisdom. I discovered the means to do such a thing, as you see. I am, essentially, pure mind. I can transfer myself from one body to another, with some effort, and thus am immortal. Efforts have been made to extinguish me, over the millennia, but they have never been successful. It would have involved the destruction of too much. Therefore I have, generally speaking, been allowed to continue my existence and my experiments. My wisdom has grown. I control both Life and Death. I can destroy and I can bring back to life. I can give other beings immortality, if I choose. By my own mind and my own skill I have become, in short, a god. Perhaps not the most powerful of gods—but that will come eventually. Now you will understand that the gods who simply—" Shool spread his hands—"*popped* into existence—who exist only through some cosmic fluke—why, they resent me. They refuse to acknowledge my godhood. They are jealous. They would like to have done with me for I disturb their self-esteem. The Knight of the Swords is my enemy. He wishes me dead. So, you see, we have much in common, Master Corum."

"I am no 'god', Prince Shool. In fact, until recently, I had no belief in gods, either."

"The fact that you are not a god, Master Corum, is evident from your obtuseness. That is not what I meant. What I did mean was this—we are both the last representatives of races whom, for reasons of their own, the Sword Rulers decided to destroy. We are both, in their eyes, anachronisms which must be eradicated. As they replaced my folk with the Vadhagh and the Nhadragh, so they are replacing the Vadhagh and the Nhadragh with the Mabden. A similar degeneration is taking place in your people— forgive me if I associate you with the Nhadragh—as it did in mine. Like me, you have attempted to resist this, to fight against it. I chose science—you chose the sword. I will leave it to you to decide which was the wisest choice…"

"You seem somewhat petty for a god," Corum said, losing his patience. "Now…"

"I am a petty god at the moment. You will find me more lordly and benign when I achieve the position of a greater god. Will you let me continue, Master Corum? Can you not understand that I have acted, so far, out of fellow feeling for you."

"Nothing you have done so far seems to indicate your friendship."

"I said fellow feeling, not friendship. I assure you, Master Corum, I could destroy you in an instant—and your lady, too."

"I would feel more patience if I knew you had released her from that dreadful bargain she made and brought her here so that I could see for myself that she still lived and is capable of being saved."

"You will have to take my word."

"Then destroy me."

Prince Shool got up. His gestures were the testy gestures of a very old man. They did not match the youthful body at all and made the sight of him even more obscene. "You should have greater respect for me, Master Corum."

"Why is that? I have seen a few tricks and heard a great deal of pompous talk."

"I am offering you much, I warn you. Be more pleasant to me."

"What are you offering me?"

Prince Shool's eyes narrowed.

"I am offering you your life. I could take it."

"You have told me that."

"I am offering you a new hand and a new eye."

Corum's interest evidently betrayed itself, for Prince Shool chuckled.

"I am offering you the return of this Mabden female you have such a perverse affection for." Prince Shool raised his hand. "Oh, very well. I apologize. Each to his own pleasures, I suppose. I am offering you the opportunity to take vengeance on the cause of your ills…"

"Glandyth-a-Krae?"

"No, no, no! The Knight of the Swords! The Knight of the Swords! The one who allowed the Mabden to take root in the first place in this plane!"

"But what of Glandyth? I have sworn his destruction."

"You accuse *me* of pettiness. Your ambitions are tiny. With the powers I offer you, you can destroy any number of Mabden earls!"

"Continue…"

"Continue? Continue? Have I not offered you enough?"

"You do not say how you propose to make these offers into something more than so much breath."

"Oh, you are insulting! The Mabden fear me! The Mabden

gibber when I materialize myself. Some of them die of terror when I make my powers manifest!"

"I have seen too much horror of late," Prince Corum said.

"That should make no difference. Your trouble is, Vadhagh, that these horrors I employ are Mabden horrors. You associate with Mabden, but you are still a Vadhagh. The dark dreams of the Mabden frighten you less than they frighten the Mabden themselves. If you had been a Mabden, I should have had an easier task of convincing you…"

"But you could not use a Mabden for the task you have in mind," Corum said grimly. "Am I right?"

"Your brains are sharpening. That is exactly the truth. No Mabden could survive what you must survive. And I am not sure that even a Vadhagh…"

"What is the task?"

"To steal something I need if I am to develop my ambitions further."

"Could you not steal it yourself?"

"Of course not. How could I leave my island? They would destroy me then, of a certainty."

"Who would destroy you?"

"My rivals, of course—the Sword Rulers and the rest! I only survive because I protect myself with all manner of devices and spells which, though they have, at this moment, the power to break, they dare not do so for fear of the consequences. To break my spells might lead to the very dissolution of the Fifteen Planes—and the extinction of the Sword Rulers themselves. No, you must do the thieving for me. No other, in this whole plane, would have the courage—or the motivation. For if you do this thing, I will restore Rhalina to you. And, if you still wish it, you will have the power to take your vengeance on Glandyth-a-Krae.

But, I assure you, the real one to blame for the very existence of Glandyth is the Knight of the Swords, and by stealing this thing from him, you will be thoroughly avenged."

Corum said, "What must I steal?"

Shool chuckled. "His heart, Master Corum."

"You wish me to kill a god and take his heart…"

"Plainly you know nothing of gods. If you killed the Knight, the consequences would be unimaginable. He does not keep his heart in his breast. It is better guarded than that. His heart is kept on this plane. His brain is kept on another—and so on. This protects him, do you see?"

Corum sighed. "You must explain more later. Now. Release Rhalina from that ship and I will try to do what you ask of me."

"You are excessively obstinate, Master Corum!"

"If I am the only one who can help you further your ambitions, Prince Shool, then I can surely afford to be."

The young lips curled in a growl that was almost Mabden. "I am glad you are not immortal, Master Corum. Your arrogance will only plague me for a few hundred years at the most. Very well, I will show you Rhalina. I will show that she is safe. But I will not release her. I will keep her here and deliver her to you when the heart of the Knight of the Swords is brought to me."

"What use is the heart to you?"

"With it, I can bargain very well."

"You may have the ambitions of a god, Master Shool, but you have the methods of a pedlar."

"*Prince* Shool. Your insults do not touch me. Now…"

Shool disappeared behind a cloud of milky green smoke that came from nowhere. A scene formed in the smoke. Corum saw the ship of the dead and he saw the cabin. He saw the corpse of the Margrave embracing the living flesh of his wife, Rhalina, the Margravine. And Corum saw that Rhalina was shouting with horror but unable to resist.

"You said she would be unharmed! Shool! You said she would be safe!"

"So she is—in the arms of a loving husband," came an offended voice from nowhere.

"Release her, Shool!"

The scene dissolved. Rhalina stood panting and terrified in the chamber that had no door. "Corum?"

Corum ran forward and held her, but she drew away with a shudder. "Is it Corum? Are you some phantom? I made a bargain to save Corum…"

"I am Corum. In turn, I have made a bargain to save you, Rhalina."

"I had not realized it would be so foul. I did not understand the terms… He was going to…"

"Even the dead have their pleasures, Mistress Rhalina." An anthropoid creature in a green coat and breeks stood behind them. It noted Corum's astonishment with pleasure. "I have several bodies I can utilize. This was an ancestor of the Nhadragh, I think. One of those races."

"Who is it, Corum?" Rhalina asked. She drew closer to him and he held her comfortingly now. Her whole body shook. Her skin was oddly damp.

"This is Shool-an-Jyvan. He claims to be a god. It was he who saw that your Summoning was answered. He has suggested that I perform an errand for him and in return he will allow you to live safely here until I return. Then we will leave together."

"But why did he…?"

"It was not you I wanted but your lover," Shool said impatiently. "Now I have broken my promise to your husband I have lost my power over him! It is irritating."

"You have lost your power over Moidel, the Margrave?" Rhalina asked.

"Yes, yes. He is completely dead. It would be far too much effort to revive him again."

"I thank you for releasing him," Rhalina said.

"It was no wish of mine. Master Corum made me do it." Prince Shool sighed. "However, there are plenty more corpses in the sea. I shall have to find another ship, I suppose."

Rhalina fainted. Corum supported her with his good hand.

"You see," Shool said, with a trace of triumph, "the Mabden fear me excellently."

"We will need food, fresh clothing, beds and the like," Corum said, "before I will discuss anything further with you, Shool."

Shool vanished.

A moment later the large room was full of furniture and everything else Corum had desired.

Corum could not doubt Shool's powers, but he did doubt the being's sanity. He undressed Rhalina and washed her and put her into bed. She awoke then and her eyes were still full of fear, but she smiled at Corum. "You are safe now," he said. "Sleep."

And she slept.

Now Corum bathed himself and inspected the clothes that had been laid out for him. He pursed his lips as he picked up the folded garments and looked at the armour and weapons that had also been provided. They were Vadhagh clothes. There was even a scarlet robe that was almost certainly his own.

He began to consider the implications of his alliance with the strange and amoral sorcerer of Svi-an-Fanla-Brool.

THE EYE OF RHYNN
AND THE HAND OF KWLL

CORUM HAD BEEN asleep.

Now, suddenly, he was standing upright. He opened his eyes.

"Welcome to my little shop." Shool's voice came from behind him. He turned. This time he confronted a beautiful girl of about fifteen. The chuckle that came from the young throat was obscene.

Corum looked around the large room. It was dark and it was cluttered. All manner of plants and stuffed animals filled it. Books and manuscripts teetered on crazily leaning shelves. There were crystals of a peculiar colour and cut, bits of armour, jeweled swords, rotting sacks from which treasure, as well as other, nameless, substances, spilled. There were paintings and figurines, an assortment of instruments and gauges including balances and what appeared to be clocks with eccentric divisions marked in languages Corum did not know. Living creatures scuffled among the piles or chittered in corners. The place stank of dust and mould and death.

"You do not, I should think, attract many customers," Corum said.

Shool sniffed. "There are not many I should desire to serve. Now…" In his young girl's form, he went to a chest that was partially covered by the shining skins of a beast that must have been large and fierce in life. He pushed away the skins and muttered something over the chest. Of its own accord, the lid flew back. A cloud of black stuff rose from within and Shool staggered away a pace or two, waving his hands and screaming in a strange speech. The black cloud vanished. Cautiously, Shool approached the chest and peered in. He smacked his lips in satisfaction, "…here we are!"

He drew out two sacks, one smaller than the other. He held them up, grinning at Corum. "Your gifts."

"I thought you were going to restore my hand and my eye."

"Not 'restore' exactly. I am going to give you a much more useful gift than that. Have you heard of the Lost Gods?"

"I have not."

"The Lost Gods who were brothers? Their names were Lord Rhynn and Lord Kwll. They existed even before I came to grace the universe. They became involved in a struggle of some kind, the nature of which is now obscured. They vanished, whether voluntarily or involuntarily, I do not know. But they left a little of themselves behind." He held up the sacks again. "These."

Corum gestured impatiently.

Shool put out his girl's tongue and licked his girl's lips. The old eyes glittered at Corum. "The gifts I have here, they once belonged to those warring gods. I heard a legend that they fought to the death and only these remained to mark the fact that they had existed at all." He opened the smaller sack. A large jeweled object fell into his hand. He held it out for Corum to see. It was jeweled and faceted. The jewels shone with sombre colours, deep reds and blues and blacks.

"It is beautiful," said Corum, "but I…"

"Wait." Shool emptied the larger sack on the lid of the chest, which had closed. He picked up the object and displayed it.

Corum gasped. It seemed to be a gauntlet with room for five slender fingers and a thumb. It, too, was covered with strange, dark jewels.

"That gauntlet is of no use to me," Corum said. "It is for a left hand with six fingers. I have five fingers and no left hand."

"It is not a gauntlet. It is Kwll's hand. He had four, but he left one behind. Struck off by his brother, I understand…"

"Your jokes do not appeal to me, sorcerer. They are too ghoulish. Again, you waste time."

"You had best get used to my jokes, as you call them, Master Vadhagh."

"I see no reason to."

"These are the gifts. To replace your missing eye—I offer you the Eye of Rhynn. To replace your missing hand—the Hand of Kwll!"

Corum's mouth curved with nausea. "I'll have nothing of them! I want no dead being's limbs! I thought you would give me back my own! You have tricked me, sorcerer!"

"Nonsense. You do not understand the properties these things possess. They will give you greater powers than any of your race or the Mabden has ever known! The eye can see into areas of time and space never observed before by a mortal. And the hand—the hand can summon aid from those areas. You do not think I would send you into the lair of the Knight of the Swords without some supernatural aid, do you?"

"What is the extent of their powers?"

Shool shrugged his young girl's shoulders. "I have not had the opportunity to test them."

"So there could be danger in using them?"

"Why should there be?"

Corum became thoughtful. Should he accept Shool's disgusting gifts and risk the consequences in order to survive, slay Glandyth and rescue Rhalina? Or should he prepare to die now and end the whole business?

Shool said, "Think of the knowledge these gifts will bring you. Think of the things you will see on your travels. No mortal has ever been to the domain of the Knight of the Swords before! You can add much to your wisdom, Master Corum. And remember—it is the Knight who is ultimately responsible for your doom and the deaths of your folk…"

Corum drew deeply of the musty air. He made up his mind.

"Very well, I will accept your gifts."

"I am honoured," Shool said sardonically. He pointed a finger at Corum and Corum reeled backwards, fell among a pile of bones and tried to rise. But he felt drowsy. "Continue your slumbers, Master Corum," Shool said.

He was back in the room in which he had originally met Shool. There was a fierce pain in the socket of his blind eye. There was a terrible agony in the stump of his left hand. He felt drained of energy. He tried to look about him, but his vision would not clear.

He heard a scream. It was Rhalina.

"Rhalina! Where are you?"

"I—I am here—Corum. What has been done to you? Your face—your hand…"

With his right hand he reached up to touch his blind socket. Something warm shifted beneath his fingers. It was an eye! But it was an eye of an unfamiliar texture and size. He knew then that it was Rhynn's eye. His vision began to clear then.

He saw Rhalina's horrified face. She was sitting up in bed, her back stiff with horror.

He looked down at his left hand. It was of similar proportions to the old, but it was six-fingered and the skin was like that of a jeweled snake.

He staggered as he strove to accept what had happened to him. "They are Shool's gifts," he murmured inanely. "They are the Eye of Rhynn and the Hand of Kwll. They were gods—the Lost Gods, Shool said. Now I am whole again, Rhalina."

"Whole? You are something more and something less than whole, Corum. Why did you accept such terrible gifts? They are evil. They will destroy you!"

"I accepted them so that I might accomplish the task that Shool has set me, and thus gain the freedom of us both. I accepted them so that I might seek out Glandyth and, if possible, strangle him with this alien hand. I accepted them because if I did not accept them, I would perish."

"Perhaps," she said softly, "it would be better for us to perish."

BEYOND THE FIFTEEN PLANES

"WHAT POWERS I have, Master Corum! I have made myself a god and I have made you a demigod. They will have us in their legends soon."

"You are already in their legends." Corum turned to confront Shool who had appeared in the room in the guise of a bearlike creature wearing an elaborate plumed helmet and trews. "And for that matter so are the Vadhagh."

"We'll have our own cycle soon, Master Corum. That is what I meant to say. How do you feel?"

"There is still some pain in my wrist and in my head."

"But no sign of a join, eh? I am a master surgeon! The grafting was perfect and accomplished with the minimum of spells!"

"I see nothing with the Eye of Rhynn, however," Corum said. "I am not sure it works, sorcerer."

Shool rubbed his paws together. "It will take time before your brain is accustomed to it. Here, you will need this, too." He produced something resembling a miniature shield of jewels and enamelwork with a strap attached to it. "It is to put over your new eye."

"And blind myself again!"

"Well, you do not want to be forever peering into those worlds beyond the Fifteen Planes, do you?"

"You mean the eye only sees there?"

"No. It sees here, too, but not always in the same kind of perspective."

Corum frowned suspiciously at the sorcerer. The action made him blink. Suddenly, through his new eye, he saw many new images, while still staring at Shool with his ordinary eye. They were dark images and they shifted until eventually one predominated.

"Shool! What is this world?"

"I am not sure. Some say there are another Fifteen Planes which are a kind of distorted mirror image of our own planes. That could be such a place, eh?"

Things boiled and bubbled, appeared and disappeared. Creatures crept upon the scene and then crept back again. Flames curled, land turned to liquid, strange beasts grew to huge proportions and shrank again, flesh seemed to flow and reform.

"I am glad I do not belong to that world," Corum murmured. "Here, Shool, give me the shield."

He took the thing from the sorcerer and positioned it over the eye. The scenes faded and now he saw only Shool and Rhalina—but with both eyes.

"Ah, I did not point out that the shield protects you from visions of the other worlds, not of this one."

"What did you see, Corum?" Rhalina asked quietly.

He shook his head. "Nothing I could easily describe."

Rhalina looked at Shool. "I wish you would take back your gifts, Prince Shool. Such things are not for mortals."

Shool grimaced. "He is not a mortal now. I told you, he is a demigod."

"And what will the gods think of that?"

"Well, naturally, some of them will be displeased if they ever discover Master Corum's new state of being. I think it unlikely, however."

Rhalina said grimly, "You talk of these matters too lightly, sorcerer. If Corum does not understand the implications of what you have done to him, I do. There are laws which mortals must obey. You have transgressed those laws and you will be punished—as your creations will be punished and destroyed!"

Shool waved his bear's arms dismissively. "You forget that I have a great deal of power. I shall soon be in a position to defy any god upstart enough to lock swords with me."

"You are insane with pride," she said. "You are only a mortal sorcerer!"

"Be silent, Mistress Rhalina! Be silent for I can send you to a far worse fate than that which you have just escaped! If Master Corum here were not useful to me, you would both be enjoying some foul form of suffering even now. Watch your tongue. Watch your tongue!"

"We are wasting time again," Corum put in. "I wish to get my task over with so that Rhalina and I can leave this place."

Shool calmed down, turned and said, "You are a fool to give so much for this creature. She, like all her kind, fears knowledge, fears the deep, dark wisdom that brings power."

"We'll discuss the heart of the Knight of the Swords," Corum said. "How do I steal it?"

"Come," said Shool.

* * *

They stood in a garden of monstrous blossoms that gave off an almost overpoweringly sweet scent. The sun was red in the sky above them. The leaves of the plants were dark, near black. They rustled.

Shool had returned to his earlier form of a youth dressed in a flowing blue robe. He led Corum along a path.

"This garden I have cultivated for millennia. It has many peculiar plants. Filling most of the island not filled by my castle, it serves a useful purpose. It is a peaceful place in which to relax, it is hard for any unwanted guests to find their way through."

"Why is the island called the Home of the Gorged God?"

"I named it that—after the being from whom I inherited it. Another god used to dwell here, you see, and all feared him. Looking for a safe place where I could continue with my studies, I found the island. But I had heard that a fearsome god inhabited it and, naturally, I was wary. I had only a fraction of my present wisdom then, being little more than a few centuries old, so I knew that I did not have the power to destroy a god."

A huge orchid reached out and stroked Corum's new hand. He pulled it away.

"Then how did you take over this island?" he asked Shool.

"I heard that the god ate children. One a day was sacrificed to him by the ancestors of those you call the Nhadragh. Having plenty of money it occurred to me to buy a good number of children and feed them to him all at once, to see what would happen."

"What did happen?"

"He gobbled them all and fell into a gorged slumber."

"And you crept up and killed him!"

"No such thing! I captured him. He is still in one of his own dungeons somewhere, though he is no longer the fine being he was when I inherited his palace. He was only a little god, of course, but some relative to the Knight of the Swords. That is another reason why the Knight, or any of the others, does not trouble me too much, for I hold Pilproth prisoner."

"To destroy your island would be to destroy their brother."

"Quite."

"And that is another reason why you must employ me to do this piece of thievery. You are afraid that if you leave they will be able to extinguish you."

"Afraid? Not at all. But I exercise a reasonable degree of caution. That is why I still exist."

"Where is the heart of the Knight of the Swords?"

"Well, it lies beyond the Thousand League Reef, of which you have doubtless heard."

"I believe I read a reference to it in some old Geography. It lies to the north, does it not?" Corum untangled a vine from his leg.

"It does."

"Is that all you can tell me?"

"Beyond the Thousand League Reef is a place called Urde that is sometimes land and sometimes water. Beyond that is the desert called Dhroonhazat. Beyond the desert are the Flamelands where dwells the Blind Queen, Ooresé. And beyond the Flamelands is the Ice Wilderness, where the Brikling wander."

Corum paused to peel a sticky leaf from his face. The thing seemed to have tiny red lips which kissed him. "And beyond that?" he asked sardonically.

"Why, beyond that is the domain of the Knight of the Swords."

"These strange lands. On which plane are they situated?"

"On all five where the Knight has influence. Your power to move through the planes will be of no great use to you, I regret."

"I am not sure I still have that power. If you speak truth, the

Knight of the Swords has been taking it away from the Vadhagh."

"Worry not, you have powers that are just as good." Shool reached over and patted Corum's strange new hand.

That hand was now responding like an ordinary limb. From curiosity, Corum used it to lift the jeweled patch that covered his jeweled eye. He gasped and lowered the patch again quickly.

Shool said, "What did you see?"

"I saw a place."

"Is that all?"

"A land over which a black sun burned. Light rose from the ground, but the black sun's rays almost extinguished it. Four figures stood before me. I glimpsed their faces and..." Corum licked his lips. "I could look no longer."

"We touch on so many planes," Shool mused. "The horrors that exist and we only sometimes catch sight of them—in dreams, for instance. However, you must learn to confront those faces and all the other things you see with your new eye, if you are to use your powers to the full."

"It disturbs me, Shool, to know that those dark, evil planes do exist and that around me lurk so many monstrous creatures, separated only by some thin, astral fabric."

"I have learned to live knowing such things—and using such things. You become used to almost everything in a few millennia."

Corum pulled a creeper from around his waist. "Your garden plants seem overfriendly."

"They are affectionate. They are my only real friends. But it is interesting that they like you. I tend to judge a being on how my plants react to him. Of course, they are hungry, poor things. I must induce a ship or two to put in to the island soon. We need meat. Meat. All this preparation has made me forgetful of my regular duties."

"You still have not described very closely how I may find the Knight of the Swords."

"You are right. Well, the Knight lives in a palace on top of a mountain that is in the very centre of both this planet and the Five Planes. In the topmost tower of that palace he keeps his heart. It is well guarded, I understand."

"And is that all you know? You do not know the nature of this protection?"

"I am employing you, Master Corum, because you have a few more brains, a jot more resilience and a fraction more imagination and courage than the Mabden. It will be up to you to discover what is the nature of his protection. You may rely upon one thing, however."

"What is it, Master Shool?"

"Prince Shool. You may rely upon the fact that he will not be expecting any kind of attack from a mortal such as yourself. Like the Vadhagh, Master Corum, the Sword Rulers grow complacent. We all climb up. We all fall down." Shool chuckled. "And the planes go on turning, eh?"

"And when you have climbed up, will you not fall down?"

"Doubtless—in a few billennia. Who knows? I could rise so high I could control the whole movement of the multiverse. I could be the first truly omniscient and omnipotent god. Oh, what games I could play!"

"We studied little of mysticism among the Vadhagh folk," Corum put in, "but I understood all gods to be omniscient and omnipotent."

"Only on very limited levels. Some gods—the Mabden pantheon such as the Dog and the Horned Bear—are more or less omniscient concerning the affairs of Mabden and they can, if they wish, control those affairs to a large degree. But they know nothing of my affairs and even less of those of the Knight of the Swords, who knows most things, save those that happen upon my well-protected island. This is an Age of Gods, I am afraid, Master Corum. There are many, big and small, and they crowd the universe. Once it was not so. Sometimes, I suspect, the universe manages with none at all!"

"I had thought that."

"It could come to pass. It is thought," Shool tapped his skull, "that creates gods and gods who create thought. There must be periods when thought—which I sometimes consider overrated—does not exist. Its existence or lack of it does not concern the universe, after all. But if I had the power—I would *make* the universe concerned!" Shool's eyes shone. "I would alter its very nature! I would change all the conditions! You are wise to aid me, Master Corum."

Corum jerked his head back as something very much like a gigantic mauve tulip, but with teeth, snapped at him.

"I doubt it, Shool. But then I have no choice."

"Indeed, you have not. Or, at least, your choice is much limited. It is the ambition I hold not to be forced to make choices, on however large a scale, which drives me on, Master Corum."

"Aye," nodded Corum ironically. "We are all mortal."

"Speak for yourself, Master Corum!"

BOOK THREE

IN WHICH PRINCE CORUM ACHIEVES
THAT WHICH IS BOTH IMPOSSIBLE
AND UNWELCOME

THE WADING GOD

CORUM'S LEAVE-TAKING FROM Rhalina had not been easy. It had been full of tension. There had been no love in her eyes as he had embraced her, only concern for him and fear for both of them.

This had disturbed him, but there had been nothing he could do.

Shool had given him a quaintly shaped boat and he had sailed away. Now sea stretched in all directions. With a lodestone to guide him, Corum sailed north for the Thousand League Reef.

Corum knew that he was mad, in Vadhagh terms. But he supposed that he was sane enough in Mabden terms. And this was, after all, now a Mabden world. He must learn to accept its peculiar disorders as normal, if he were going to survive. And there were many reasons why he wished to survive, Rhalina not least among them. He was the last of the Vadhagh, yet he could not believe it. The powers available to sorcerers like Shool might be controlled by others. The nature of time could be tampered with. The circling planes could be halted in their course, perhaps reversed. The events of the past year could be changed, perhaps eradicated completely. Corum proposed to live and, in living, to learn.

And if he learned enough, perhaps he would gain sufficient power to fulfill his ambitions and restore a world to the Vadhagh and the Vadhagh to the world.

It would be just, he thought.

The boat was of beaten metal on which were many raised and asymmetrical designs. It gave off a faint glow which offered Corum both heat and light during the nights, for the sailing was long. Its single mast bore a single square sail of samite smeared with a strange substance that also shone and turned, without Corum's guidance, to catch any wind. Corum sat in the boat wrapped in his scarlet robe, his war-gear laid beside him, his silver helm upon his head, his double byrnie covering him from throat to knee. From time to time he would hold up his lodestone by its string. The stone was shaped like an arrow and the head pointed always north.

He thought much of Rhalina and his love for her. Such a love had never before existed between a Vadhagh and a Mabden. His own folk might have considered his feelings for Rhalina degenerate, much as a Mabden would suspect such feelings in a man for his mare, but he was attracted to her more than he had been attracted to any Vadhagh woman and he knew that her intelligence was a match for his. It was her moods he found hard to understand—her intimations of doom—her superstition.

Yet Rhalina knew this world better than he. It could be that she was right to entertain such thoughts. His lessons were not yet over.

On the third night, Corum slept, his new hand on the boat's tiller, and in the morning he was awakened by bright sunshine in his eyes.

Ahead lay the Thousand League Reef.

It stretched from end to end of the horizon and there seemed to be no gap in the sharp fangs of rock that rose from the foaming sea.

Shool had warned him that few had ever found a passage through the reef and now he could understand why. The reef was unbroken. It seemed not of natural origin at all, but to have been placed there by some entity as a bastion against intruders. Perhaps the Knight of the Swords had built it.

Corum decided to sail in an easterly direction along the reef, hoping to find somewhere where he could land the boat and perhaps drag it overland to the waters that lay beyond the reef.

He sailed for another four days, without sleep, and the reef offered neither a passage through nor a place to land.

A light mist, tinged pink by the sun, now covered the water in all directions and Corum kept away from the reef by using his lodestone and by listening for the sounds of the surf on the rocks. He drew out his maps, pricked out on skin, and tried to judge his position. The maps were crude and probably inaccurate, but they were the best Shool had had. He was nearing a narrow channel between the reef and a land marked on the map as Khoolocrah. Shool had been unable to tell him much about the land, save that a race called the Ragha-da-Kheta lived thereabouts.

In the light from the boat, he peered at the maps, hoping to distinguish some gap in the reef marked there, but there was none.

Then the boat began to rock rapidly and Corum glanced about him, seeking the source of this sudden eddy. Far away, the surf boomed, but then he heard another sound, to the south of him, and he looked there.

The sound was a regular rushing and slapping noise, like that of a man wading through a stream. Was this some beast of the sea? The Mabden seemed to fear many such monsters. Corum clung desperately to the sides, trying to keep the boat on course away from the rocks, but the waves increased their agitation.

And the sound came closer.

Corum picked up his long, strong sword and readied himself.

He saw something in the mist then. It was a tall, bulky shape—the outline of a man. And the man was dragging something behind him. A fishing net! Were the waters so shallow, then? Corum leaned over the side and lowered his sword, point downward, into the sea. It did not touch bottom. He could make out the ocean floor a long way below him. He looked back at the figure. Now he realized that his eyes and the mist had played tricks on him. The figure was still some distance from him and it was gigantic—far huger than the Giant of Laahr. This was what made the waves so large. This was why the boat rocked so.

Corum made to call out, to ask the gigantic creature to move away lest he sink the boat, then he thought better of it. Beings like this were considered to think less kindly of mortals than did the Giant of Laahr.

Now the giant, still cloaked in mist, changed his course, still fishing. He was behind Corum's boat and he trudged on through the water, dragging his nets behind him.

The wash sent the boat flying away from the Thousand League Reef, heading almost due east, and there was nothing Corum could do to stop it. He fought with the sail and the tiller, but they would not respond. It was as if he was borne on a river rushing towards a chasm. The giant had set up a current which he could not fight.

There was nothing for it but to allow the boat to bear him where it would. The giant had long since disappeared in the mist, heading towards the Thousand League Reef where perhaps he lived.

Like a shark pouncing on its prey, the little boat moved, until suddenly it broke through the mist into hot sunshine.

And Corum saw a coast. Cliffs rushed at him.

2

TEMGOL-LEP

DESPERATELY CORUM TRIED to turn the boat away from the cliffs. His six-fingered left hand gripped the tiller and his right hand tugged at the sail.

Then there was a grinding sound. A shudder ran through the metal boat and it began to keel over. Corum grabbed at his weapons and managed to seize them before he was flung overboard and carried on by the wash. He gasped as water filled his mouth. He felt his body scrape on shingle and he tried to stagger upright as the current began to retreat. He saw a rock and grasped it, dropping his bow and his quiver of arrows which were instantly swept away.

The sea retreated. He looked back and saw that his upturned boat had gone with it. He let go of the rock and climbed to his feet, buckling his sword belt around his waist, straightening his helmet on his head, a sense of failure gradually creeping through him.

He walked a few paces up the beach and sat down beneath the

tall, black cliff. He was stranded on a strange shore, his boat was gone and his goal now lay on the other side of an ocean.

At that moment Corum did not care. Thoughts of love, of hatred, of vengeance disappeared. He felt that he had left them all behind in the dreamworld that was Svi-an-Fanla-Brool. All he had left of that world was the six-fingered hand and the jeweled eye.

Reminded of the eye and what it had witnessed, he shivered. He reached up and touched the patch that covered it.

And then he knew that by accepting Shool's gifts, he had accepted the logic of Shool's world. He could not escape from it now.

Sighing, he got up and peered at the cliff. It was unscaleable. He began to walk along the grey shingle, hoping to discover a place where he could climb to the top of the cliff and inspect the land in which he found himself.

He took a gauntlet given him by Shool and drew it over his hand. He remembered what Shool had told him, before he left, about the powers of the hand. He still only half-believed Shool's words and he was unwilling to test their veracity.

For more than an hour he trudged along the shore until he moved round a headland and saw a bay whose sides sloped gently upward and would be easily scaled. The tide was beginning to come in and would soon cover the beach. He began to run.

He reached the slopes and paused, panting. He had found safety in time. The sea had already covered the largest part of the beach. He climbed to the top of the slope and he saw the city.

It was a city of domes and minarets that blazed white in the light of the sun, but as he inspected it more closely Corum saw that the towers and domes were not white, but comprised of a multicoloured mosaic. He had seen nothing like it.

He debated whether to avoid the city or approach it. If the people of the city were friendly, he might be able to get their help to find another boat. If they were Mabden, then they were probably unfriendly.

Were these the Ragha-da-Kheta people mentioned on his maps? He felt for his pouch, but the maps had gone with the boat, as had his lodestone. Despair returned.

He set off towards the city.

Corum had travelled less than a mile before the bizarre cavalry came racing towards him—warriors mounted on long-necked speckled beasts with curling horns and wattles like those of a lizard. The spindly legs moved swiftly, however, and soon Corum could see that the warriors were also very tall and extremely thin, but with small, rounded heads and round eyes. These were not Mabden, but they were like no race he had ever heard of.

He stopped and waited. There was nothing else he could do until he discovered if they were his enemies or not.

Swiftly, they surrounded him, peering down at him through their huge, staring eyes. Their noses and their mouths were also round and their expressions were ones of permanent surprise.

"Olanja ko?" said one wearing an elaborate cloak and hood of bright feathers and holding a club fashioned like the claw of a giant bird. "Olanja ko, drajer?"

Using the Low Speech of the Vadhagh and the Nhadragh, which was the common tongue of the Mabden, Corum replied, "I do not understand this language."

The creature in the feather cloak cocked his head to one side and closed his mouth. The other warriors, all dressed and armed similarly, though not as elaborately, muttered among themselves.

Corum pointed roughly southwards. "I come from across the sea." Now he used Middle Speech which Vadhagh and Nhadragh had spoken, but not Mabden.

The rider leaned forward as if this sound was more familiar to him, but then he shook his head, understanding none of the words.

"Olanja ko?"

Corum also shook his head. The warrior looked puzzled and made a delicate scratching gesture at his cheek. Corum could not interpret the gesture.

The leader pointed at one of his followers. "Mor naffa!" The man dismounted and waved one of his spindly arms at Corum, gesturing that he climb on the long-necked beast.

With some difficulty, Corum managed to swing himself into the narrow saddle and sit there, feeling extreme discomfort.

"Hoj!" The leader waved to his men and turned his mount back towards the city. "Hoj—ala!"

The beasts jogged off, leaving the remaining warrior to make his way back to the city on foot.

The city was surrounded by a high wall patterned with many geometric designs of a thousand colours. They entered it through a tall, narrow gate, moved through a series of walls that were probably designed as a simple maze, and began to ride along a broad avenue of blooming trees towards a palace that lay at the centre of the city.

Reaching the gates of the palace, they all dismounted and servants, as thin and tall as the warriors, with the same astonished round faces, took away the mounts. Corum was led through the gates, up a staircase of more than a hundred steps, into an enclave. The designs on the walls of the palace were less colourful but more elaborate than those on the outer walls of the city. These were chiefly in gold, white and pale blue. Although faintly barbaric, the workmanship was beautiful and Corum admired it.

They crossed the enclave and entered a courtyard that was surrounded by an enclosed walk and had a fountain in its centre.

Under an awning was a large chair with a tapering back. The chair was made of gold and a design was picked out upon it in rubies. The warriors escorting Corum came to a halt and almost immediately a figure emerged from the interior. He had a huge, high headdress of peacock feathers, a great cloak, also of many brilliant feathers, and a kilt of thin gold cloth. He took his place on the throne. This, then, was the ruler of the city.

The leader of the warriors and his monarch conversed briefly in their own language and Corum waited patiently, not wishing to behave in any way that these people would judge to be unfriendly.

At length the two creatures stopped conversing. The monarch addressed Corum. He seemed to speak several different tongues until at length Corum heard him say, in a strange accent:

"Are you of the Mabden race?"

It was the old speech of the Nhadragh, which Corum had learned as a child.

"I am not," he replied haltingly.

"But you are not Nhedregh."

"Yes—I am not—'Nhedregh'. You know of that folk?"

"Two of them lived among us some centuries since. What race are you?"

"The Vadhagh."

The king sucked at his lips and smacked them. "The enemy, yes, of the Nhedregh?"

"Not now."

"Not now?" The king frowned.

"All the Vadhagh save me are dead," Corum explained. "And what is left of those you call Nhedregh have become degenerate slaves of the Mabden."

"But the Mabden are barbarians!"

"Now they are very powerful barbarians."

The king nodded. "This was predicted." He studied Corum closely. "Why are you not dead?"

"I chose not to die."

"No choice was yours if Arioch decided."

"Who is 'Arioch'?"

"The god."

"Which god?"

"The god who rules our destinies. Duke Arioch of the Swords."

"The Knight of the Swords?"

"I believe he is known by that title in the distant south." The king seemed deeply disturbed now. He licked his lips. "I am King Temgol-Lep. This is my city, Arke." He waved his thin hand. "These are my people, the Ragha-da-Kheta. This land is called Khoolocrah. We, too, soon shall die."

"Why so?"

"It is Mabden time. Arioch decides." The king shrugged his narrow shoulders. "Arioch decides. Soon the Mabden will come and destroy us."

"You will fight them, of course."

"No. It is Mabden time. Arioch commands. He lets the Ragha-da-Kheta live longer because they obey him, because they do not resist him. But soon we shall die."

Corum shook his head. "Do you not think that Arioch is unjust to destroy you thus?"

"Arioch decides."

It occurred to Corum that these people had not been so fatalistic once. Perhaps they, too, were in a process of degeneration, caused by the Knight of the Swords.

"Why should Arioch destroy so much beauty and learning as you have here?"

"Arioch decides."

King Temgol-Lep seemed to be more familiar with the Knight of the Swords and his plans than anyone Corum had yet met. Living so much closer to his domain, perhaps they had seen him.

"Has Arioch told you this himself?"

"He has spoken through our wise ones."

"And the wise ones—they are certain of Arioch's will?"

"They are certain."

Corum sighed. "Well, I intend to resist his plans. I do not find them agreeable!"

King Temgol-Lep drew his lids over his eyes and trembled slightly. The warriors looked at him nervously. Evidently they recognized that the king was displeased.

"I will speak no more about Arioch," King Temgol-Lep said. "But as our guest we must entertain you. You will drink some wine with us."

"I will drink some wine. I thank you." Corum would have preferred food to begin with, but he was still cautious of giving offence to the Ragha-da-Kheta, who might yet supply him with the boat he needed.

The king spoke to some servants who were waiting in the shadows near the door into the palace. They went inside.

Soon they returned with a tray on which were tall, thin goblets and a golden jug. The king reached out and took the tray in his own hands, balancing it on his knee. Gravely, he poured wine into one of the cups and handed it to Corum.

Corum stretched out his left hand to receive the goblet.

The hand quivered.

Corum tried to control it, but it knocked the goblet away. The king looked startled and began to speak.

The hand plunged forward and its six fingers seized the king's throat.

King Temgol-Lep gurgled and kicked as Corum tried to pull the Hand of Kwll away. But the fingers were locked on the throat. Corum could feel himself squeezing the life from the king.

Corum shouted for help before he realized that the warriors thought that he was attacking the king on his own volition. He drew his sword and hacked around him as they attacked with their oddly wrought clubs. They were plainly unused to battle, for their actions were clumsy and without proper coordination.

Suddenly the hand released King Temgol-Lep and Corum saw that he was dead.

His new hand had murdered a kindly and innocent creature! And it had ruined his chances of getting help from the Ragha-da-Kheta. It might even have killed him, for the warriors were very numerous.

Standing over the corpse of the king, he swept his sword this way and that, striking limbs from bodies, cutting into heads. Blood gushed everywhere and covered him, but he fought on.

Then, suddenly, there were no more living warriors. He stood in the courtyard while the gentle sun beat down and the fountain played and he looked at all the corpses. He raised his gauntleted alien hand and spat on it.

"Oh, evil thing! Rhalina was right! You have made me a murderer!"

But the hand was his again, it had no life of its own. He flexed the six fingers. It was now like any ordinary limb.

Save for the splashing of the water from the fountain, the courtyard was silent.

Corum looked back at the dead king and shuddered. He raised his sword. He would cut the Hand of Kwll from him. Better to be crippled than to be the slave of so evil a thing!

And then the ground fell away from him and he plunged downwards to fall with a crash upon the back of a beast that spat and clawed at him.

THE DARK THINGS COME

CORUM SAW DAYLIGHT above and then the flagstone slid back and he was in darkness with the beast that dwelt in the pit beneath the courtyard. It was snarling in a corner somewhere. He prepared to defend himself against it.

Then the snarling stopped and there was silence for a moment. Corum waited.

He heard a shuffling. He saw a spark. The spark became a flame. The flame came from a wick that burned in a clay vessel full of oil.

The clay vessel was held by a filthy hand. And the hand belonged to a hairy creature whose eyes were full of anger.

"Who are you?" Corum said.

The creature shuffled again and placed the crude lamp in a niche on the wall. Corum saw that the chamber was covered in dirty straw. There was a pitcher and a plate and, at the far end, a heavy iron door. The place reeked of human excrement.

"Can you understand me?" Corum still spoke the Nhadragh tongue.

"Stop your gabbling." The creature spoke distantly, as if he did not expect Corum to know what he was saying. He had spoken in the Low Speech. "You will be like me soon."

Corum made no reply. He sheathed his sword and walked about the cell, inspecting it. There seemed no obvious way to escape. Above him he heard footsteps on the flagstones of the courtyard. He heard, quite clearly, the voices of the Ragha-da-Kheta. They were agitated, almost hysterical.

The creature cocked his head and listened.

"So that is what happened," he mused, staring at Corum and grinning to himself. "You killed the feeble little coward, eh? Hm, well I don't resent your company nearly so much. Though your stay will be short, I fear. I wonder how they will destroy you…"

Corum listened in silence, still not revealing that he understood the creature's words. He heard the sound of the corpses being dragged away overhead. More voices came and went.

"Now they are in a quandary," chuckled the creature. "They are only good at killing by stealth. What did they try to do to you, my friend, poison you? That's the way they usually get rid of those they fear."

Poison? Corum frowned. Had the wine been poisoned? He looked at the hand. Had it—*known*? Was it in some way sentient?

He decided to break his silence. "Who are you?" he said in the Low Speech.

The creature began to laugh. "So you can understand me! Well, since you are my guest, I feel you should answer my questions first. You look like a Vadhagh to me, yet I thought all the Vadhagh perished long since. Name yourself and your folk, friend."

Corum said, "I am Corum Jhaelen Irsei—the Prince in the

Scarlet Robe. And I am the last of the Vadhagh."

"And I am Hanafax of Pengarde, something of a soldier, something of a priest, something of an explorer—and something of a wretch, as you see. I hail from a land called Lywm-an-Esh—a land far to the west where…"

"I know of Lywm-an-Esh. I have been a guest of the Margravine of the east."

"What? Does that Margravate still exist? I had heard it had been washed away by the encroaching seas long since!"

"It may be destroyed by now. The Pony Tribes…"

"By Urleh! Pony Tribes! It is something from the histories."

"How come you to be so far from your own land, Sir Hanafax?"

"It's a long tale, Prince Corum. Arioch—as he is called here—does not smile on the folk of Lywm-an-Esh. He expects all the Mabden to do his work for him—chiefly in the reduction of the older races, such as your own. As you doubtless know, our folk have had no interest in destroying these races, for they have never harmed us. But Urleh is a kind of vassal deity to the Knight of the Swords. It was Urleh that I served as a priest. Well, it seems that Arioch grows impatient (for reasons of his own) and commands Urleh to command the people of Lywm-an-Esh to embark on a crusade, to travel far to the west where a seafolk dwell. These folk are only about fifty in all and live in castles built into coral. They are called the Shalafen. Urleh gave me Arioch's command. I decided to believe that this was a false command—coming from another entity unfriendly to Urleh. My luck, which was never of the best, changed greatly then. There was a murder. I was blamed. I fled my lands and stole a ship. After several somewhat dull adventures, I found myself among this twittering people who so patiently await Arioch's destruction. I attempted to band them together against Arioch. They offered me wine, which I refused.

They seized me and placed me here, where I have been for more than a few months."

"What will they do with you?"

"I cannot say. Hope that I die eventually, I suppose. They are a misguided folk and a little stupid, but they are not by nature cruel. Yet their terror of Arioch is so great that they dare not do anything that might offend him. In this way they hope he will let them live a year or two longer."

"And you do not know how they will deal with me? I killed their king, after all."

"That is what I was considering. The poison has failed. They would be very reluctant to use violence on you themselves. We shall have to see."

"I have a mission to accomplish," Corum told him. "I cannot afford to wait."

Hanafax grinned. "I think you will have to, friend Corum! I am something of a sorcerer, as I told you. I have a few tricks, but none will work in this place, I know not why. And if sorcery cannot aid us, what can?"

Corum raised his alien hand and stared at it thoughtfully.

Then he looked into the hairy face of his fellow prisoner. "Have you ever heard of the Hand of Kwll?"

Hanafax frowned. "Aye… I believe I have. The sole remains of a god, one of two brothers, who had some sort of feud… A legend, of course, like so many—"

Corum held up his left hand. "This is the Hand of Kwll. It was given me by a sorcerer, along with this eye—the Eye of Rhynn—and both have great powers, I am told."

"You do not know?"

"I have had no opportunity to test them."

Hanafax seemed disturbed. "Yet such powers are too great for a mortal, I would have thought. The consequences of using them would be monstrous…"

"I do not believe I have any choice. I have decided. I will call upon the powers of the Hand of Kwll and the Eye of Rhynn!"

"I trust you will remind them that I am on your side, Prince Corum."

Corum stripped the gauntlet from his six-fingered hand. He was shivering with the tension. Then he pushed the patch up to his forehead.

He began to see the darker planes. Again he saw the landscape on which a black sun shone. Again he saw the four cowled figures.

And this time he stared into their faces.

He screamed.

But he could not name the reason for his terror.

He looked again.

The Hand of Kwll stretched out towards the figures. Their heads moved as they saw the hand. Their terrible eyes seemed to draw all the heat from his body, all the vitality from his soul. But he continued to look at them.

The hand beckoned.

The dark figures moved towards Corum.

He heard Hanafax say, "I see nothing. What are you summoning? What do you see?"

Corum ignored him. He was sweating now and every limb save the Hand of Kwll was shaking.

From beneath their robes the four figures drew huge scythes.

Corum moved numbed lips. "Here. Come to this plane. Obey me."

They came nearer and seemed to pass through a swirling curtain of mist.

Then Hanafax cried out in terror and disgust. "Gods! They are things from the Pits of the Dog! Shefanhow!" He jumped behind Corum. "Keep them off me, Vadhagh! Aah!"

Hollow voices issued from the strangely distorted mouths: "Master. We will do your will. We will do the will of Kwll."

"Destroy that door!" Corum commanded.

"Will we have our prize, master?"

"What prize is that?"

"A life for each of us, master."

Corum shuddered. "Aye, very well, when they're to spare, you'll have your prize."

The scythes rose up and the door fell down and the four creatures that were truly 'Shefanhow' led the way into a narrow passage.

"My kite!" Hanafax murmured to Corum. "We can escape on that."

"A kite?"

"Aye. It flies and can take both of us."

The Shefanhow marched ahead. From them radiated a force that froze the skin.

They mounted some steps and another door was burst by the scythes of the cloaked creatures. There was daylight.

They found themselves in the main courtyard of the palace.

From all sides came warriors. This time they did not seem so reluctant to kill Corum and Hanafax, but they paused when they saw the four cloaked beings.

"There are your prizes," Corum said. "Take as many as you will and then return to whence you came."

The scythes whirled in the sunshine. The Ragha-da-Kheta fell back screaming.

The screaming grew louder.

The four began to titter. Then they began to roar. Then they began to echo the screams of their victims as their scythes swung and heads sprang from necks.

Sickened, Corum and Hanafax ran through the corridors of the palace. Hanafax led the way and eventually stopped outside a door.

Everywhere now the screams sounded and the loudest screams of all were those of the four.

Hanafax forced the door open. It was dark within. He began to rummage about in the room. "This is where I was when I was their guest. Before they decided that I had offended Arioch. I came here in my kite. Now…"

Corum saw more soldiers rushing down the corridor towards them.

"Find it quickly, Hanafax," he said. He leapt out to block the corridor with his sword.

The spindly beings came to a halt and looked at his sword. They raised their own bird-claw clubs and began cautiously to advance.

Corum's sword darted out and cut a warrior's throat. He collapsed in a tangle of legs and arms. Corum struck another in the eye.

The screams were dying now. Corum's foul allies were returning to their own plane with their prizes.

Behind Corum, Hanafax was dragging forth a dusty arrangement of rods and silk. "I have it, Prince Corum. Give me a short while to remember the spell I need."

Rather than being frightened by the deaths of their comrades, the Ragha-da-Kheta seemed spurred on to fight more fiercely. Partly protected by a little mound of the slain, Corum fought on.

Hanafax began to call out something in a strange tongue. Corum felt a wind rise that ruffled his scarlet robe. Something grabbed him from behind and then he was rising into the air, over the heads of the Ragha-da-Kheta, speeding along the corridor and into the open.

He looked down nervously.

The city was rushing past below them.

Hanafax dragged him into the box of yellow-and-green silk. Corum was sure he would fall, but the kite held.

The ragged, unkempt figure beside him was grinning.

"So the will of Arioch can be denied," Corum said.

"Unless we are his instruments in this," said Hanafax, his grin fading.

IN THE FLAMELANDS

ORUM GOT USED to the flight, though he still felt uncomfortable. Hanafax hummed to himself while he chopped at his hair and whiskers until a handsome, youngish face was revealed. Apparently without concern, he discarded his rags and drew on a clean doublet and pair of breeks he had brought with him in his bundle.

"I feel a thousand times improved. I thank you, Prince Corum, for visiting the City of Arke before I had entirely rotted away!" Corum had discovered that Hanafax could not sustain his moods of introspection but was naturally of a cheerful disposition.

"Where is this flying thing taking us, Sir Hanafax?"

"Ah, there's the problem," Hanafax said. "It is why I have found myself in more trouble than I sought. I cannot—um—*guide* the kite. It flies where it will."

They were over the sea now.

Corum clung to the struts and fixed his eyes ahead of him while Hanafax began a song which was not complimentary either to Arioch or the Dog God of the eastern Mabden folk.

Then Corum saw something below and he said dryly, "I would advise you to forget the insults to Arioch. We appear to be flying over the Thousand League Reef. As I understand it, his domain lies somewhere beyond that."

"A fair distance, though. I hope the kite brings us down soon."

They reached the coast. Corum screwed up his eyes as he tried to make it out. Some of the time it seemed to consist of water alone—a kind of huge inland sea—and some of the time the water vanished completely and only land could be seen. It was shifting all the time.

"Is that Urde, Sir Hanafax?"

"I think it must be the place 'Urde' by its position and appearance. Unstable matter, Prince Corum, created by the Chaos Lords."

"The Chaos Lords? I have not heard that term used before."

"Have you not? Well, it is their will that rules you. Arioch is one of them. Long since there was a war between the forces of Order and the forces of Chaos. The forces of Chaos won and came to dominate the Fifteen Planes and, as I understand it, much that lies beyond them. Some say that Order was defeated completely and all her gods vanished. They say the Cosmic Balance tipped too far in one direction and that is why there are so many arbitrary events taking place in the world. They say that once the world was *round* instead of dish-shaped. It is hard to accept, I agree."

"Some Vadhagh legends say it was once round."

"Aye. Well, the Vadhagh began their rise just before Order was banished. That is why the Sword Rulers hate the Old Races so much. They are not their creation at all. But the Great Gods are not allowed to interfere too directly in mortal affairs, so they have worked through the Mabden, chiefly…"

"Is this the truth?"

"It is *a* truth," Hanafax shrugged. "I know other versions of the same tale. But I am inclined to believe this one."

"These Great Gods—you speak of the Sword Rulers?"

"Aye, the Sword Rulers and others. Then there are the Great Old Gods, to whom all the myriad planes of Earth are merely a tiny fragment in a greater mosaic." Hanafax shrugged. "This is the cosmology I was taught when I was a priest. I cannot vouch for its truth."

Corum frowned. He looked below and now they were crossing a bleak yellow-and-brown desert. It was the desert called Dhroonhazat and it seemed entirely waterless. By an accident of fate he was being borne towards the Knight of the Swords faster than he had expected.

Or was it an accident of fate?

Now the heat was increasing and the sand below shimmered and danced. Hanafax licked his lips. "We're getting dangerously close to the Flamelands, Prince Corum. Look."

On the horizon Corum saw a thin, flickering line of red light. The sky above it was also tinged red.

The kite sped nearer and the heat increased. To his astonishment, Corum saw that they were approaching a wall of flame that stretched as far as he could see in both directions.

"Hanafax, we shall be burned alive," he said softly.

"Aye, it seems likely."

"Is there no means of turning this kite of yours?"

"I have tried, in the past. It is not the first time it has taken me away from one danger and into a worse one…"

The wall of fire was now so close that Corum could feel its direct heat burning his face. He heard it rumble and crackle and it seemed to feed on nothing but the air itself.

"Such a thing defies nature!" he gasped.

"Is that not a fair definition of all sorcery?" Hanafax said. "This is Chaos work. The disruption of the natural harmony is, after all, their pleasure."

"Ah, this sorcery. It wearies my mind. I cannot grasp its logic."

"That is because it has none. It is arbitrary. The Lords of Chaos are the enemies of Logic, the jugglers of Truth, the moulders of Beauty. I should be surprised if they had not created these Flamelands out of some aesthetic impulse. Beauty—an ever-changing beauty—is all they live for."

"An evil beauty."

"I believe that such notions as 'good' and 'evil' do not exist for the Chaos Lords."

"I should like to make it exist for them." Corum mopped his sweating head with his coat sleeve.

"And destroy all their beauty?"

Corum darted an odd look at Hanafax. Was the Mabden on the side of the Knight? Had he, in fact, trapped Corum into accompanying him?

"There are other, quieter kinds of beauty, Sir Hanafax."

"True."

Everywhere below them now the flame yelled and leapt. The kite began to increase its height as its silk started to smoulder. Corum was certain it would soon be destroyed by the fire and they would be plunged into the depths of the flame wall.

But now they were above it and, in spite of the silk suddenly springing alive with little fires and Corum feeling he was being roasted in his armour like a turtle in its shell, they now saw the other side of the wall.

A piece of the kite fell blazing away.

Hanafax, his face a bright red, his body running with sweat, clung to a strut and gasped, "Grasp a beam, Prince Corum! Grasp a beam!"

Corum took hold of one of the beams beneath his body as the burning silk was ripped from the frame and fluttered into the fires below. The kite dipped and threatened to follow the silk. It was losing height rapidly. Corum coughed as the burning air entered his lungs. Blisters appeared on his right hand, though his left hand seemed immune.

The kite lurched and began to fall.

Corum was flung back and forth during the crazy descent, but he managed to keep his hold on the strut. Then there was a cracking sound, a mighty thump, and he lay amidst the wreckage on a surface of flat obsidian, the wall of flame behind him.

He raised his bruised body upright. It was still unbearably hot and the flames sang close to his back, rising a hundred feet or more into the air. The fused rock on which he stood was green and glistened and reflected the flame, seeming to writhe beneath his feet. A little distance to his left ran a sluggish river of molten lava, a few flames fluttering on its surface. Everywhere Corum looked was the same shining rock, the same red rivers of fire. He inspected the kite. It was completely useless. Hanafax was lying among its struts cursing it. He got up.

"Well," he kicked at the blackened, broken frame, "you'll never fly me into any more dangers!"

"I think this danger is all we need," Corum said. "It could be the last one we'll ever face."

Hanafax picked up his sword belt from the wreckage and tied it round his shoulders. "Aye, I think you could speak truth, Prince Corum. A poor place to meet one's end, eh?"

"According to some Mabden legends," Corum said, "we might already have met our ends and been consigned here. Are not certain Mabden netherworlds said to be made of eternally burning flame?"

Hanafax snorted. "In the east, perhaps. Well, we cannot go back, so I suppose we must go forward."

"I was told that an Ice Wilderness lay towards the north," Corum said. "Though how it does not melt being so near to the Flamelands, I do not know."

"Another quirk of the Lords of Chaos, doubtless."

"Doubtless."

They began to make their way over the slippery rock that burned their feet with every step, leaving the wall of flame behind them, leaping over rivulets of lava, moving so slowly and so circuitously that they were soon exhausted and paused to rest, look back at the distant flame wall, mop their brows, exchange daunted looks. Thirst now plagued them and their voices were hoarse.

"I think we are doomed, Prince Corum."

Corum nodded wearily. He looked up. Red clouds boiled above, like a dome of fire. It seemed that all the world burned.

"Have you no spells for bringing on rain, Sir Hanafax?"

"I regret not. We priests scorn such primitive tricks."

"Useful tricks. Sorcerers seem to enjoy only the spectacular."

"I am afraid it is so." Hanafax sighed. "What about your own powers? Can you not," he shuddered, "summon some kind of aid from whatever netherworld it is your horrid allies came?"

"I fear those allies are only useful in battle. I have no true conception of what they are or why they come. I have come to believe that the sorcerer who fitted me with this hand and eye had no clearer idea himself. His work was something of an experiment, it seems."

"You have noticed, I take it, that the sun does not appear

to set in the Flamelands. We can expect no night to come to relieve us."

Corum was about to reply when he saw something move on a rise of black obsidian a short distance away. "Hush, Sir Hanafax…"

Hanafax peered through the smoky heat. "What is it?"

And then they revealed themselves.

There were about a score of them, mounted on beasts whose bodies were covered in thick, scaly skin resembling plate armour. They had four short legs and cloven feet, a nest of horns jutted on heads and snouts and small red eyes gleamed at them. The riders were covered from head to foot in red garments of some shining material which hid even their faces and hands. They had long, barbed lances for weapons.

Silently, they surrounded Corum and Hanafax.

For a few moments there was silence, and then one of the riders spoke. "What do you in our Flamelands, strangers?"

"We are not here from choice," replied Corum. "An accident brought us to your country. We are peaceful."

"You are not peaceful. You bear swords."

"We did not know there were any inhabitants to these lands," Hanafax said. "We seek help. We wish to leave."

"None may leave the Flamelands save to suffer a mighty doom." The voice was sonorous, even sad. "There is only one gateway and that is through the Lion's Mouth."

"Can we not…?"

The riders began to close in. Corum and Hanafax drew their swords.

"Well, Prince Corum, it seems we are to die."

Corum's face was grim. He pushed up his eye-patch. For a moment his vision clouded and then he saw into the netherworld once again. He wondered for a moment if it would not be better to die at the hands of the Flameland dwellers but now he was looking at a cavern in which tall figures stood as if frozen.

With a shock Corum recognized them as the dead warriors of the Ragha-da-Kheta, their wounds now bloodless, their eyes glazed, their clothes and armour torn, their weapons still in their hands. They began to move towards him as his hand stretched out to summon them.

"NO! These, too, are my enemies!" Corum shouted.

Hanafax, unable to see what Corum saw, turned his head in astonishment.

The dead warriors came on. The scene behind them faded. They materialized on the obsidian rock of the Flamelands.

Corum backed away, gesticulating wildly. The Flameland warriors drew their mounts to a stop in surprise. Hanafax's face was a mask of fear.

"No! I…"

From the lips of the dead King Temgol-Lep came a whispering voice. "We serve you, master. Will you give us our prizes?"

Corum controlled himself. Slowly, he nodded. "Aye. You may take your prizes."

The long-limbed warriors turned to face the mounted warriors of the Flamelands. The beasts snorted and tried to move back but were forced to stand their ground by their riders. There were about fifty of the Ragha-da-Kheta. Dividing into groups of two or three, their clawed clubs raised, they flung themselves at the mounted beings.

Barbed lances came up and stabbed down at the Ragha-da-Kheta. Many were struck, but it did not deter them. They began to drag the struggling riders from their saddles.

Pale-faced, Corum watched. He knew now that he was consigning the Flamelands' warriors to the same netherworld from which he had summoned the Ragha-da-Kheta. And his actions had sent the Ragha-da-Kheta to that netherworld in the first place.

On the gleaming rock, around which ran rivers of red lava, the ghastly battle continued. The clawed clubs ripped the cloaks from the riders, revealing a people whose faces were familiar.

"Stop!" Corum cried. "Stop! That is enough. Kill no more!"

Temgol-Lep turned his glazed eyes on Corum. The dead king had a barbed spear sticking completely through his body, but he seemed unaware of it. His dead lips moved. "These are our prizes, master. We cannot stop."

"But they are Vadhagh! They are like me! They are my own people!"

Hanafax put an arm on Corum's shoulder. "They are all dead now, Prince Corum."

Sobbing, Corum ran towards the corpses, inspecting the faces. They had the same long skulls, the same huge, almond eyes, the same tapering ears.

"How came Vadhagh here?" Hanafax murmured.

Now Temgol-Lep was dragging one of the corpses away, aided by two of his minions. The scaled beasts scattered, some of them splashing through the lava uncaringly.

Through the Eye of Rhynn, Corum saw the Ragha-da-Kheta pull the corpses into their cave. With a shudder, he replaced the eye-patch. Save for a few weapons and tatters of armour and clothing, save for the disappearing mounts, nothing remained of the Vadhagh of the Flamelands.

"I have destroyed my own folk!" Corum screamed. "I have consigned them to a frightful doom in that netherworld!"

"Sorcery has a way of recoiling suddenly upon its user," Hanafax said quietly. "It is an arbitrary power, as I said."

Corum wheeled on Hanafax. "Stop your prattling, Mabden! Do you not realize what I have done?"

Hanafax nodded soberly. "Aye. But it *is* done, is it not? Our lives are saved."

"Now I add fratricide to my crimes." Corum fell to his knees, dropping his sword on the rock. And he wept.

"Who weeps?"

It was a woman's voice. A sad voice.

"Who weeps for Cira-an-Venl, the Lands That Are Now Flame? Who remembers her sweet meadows and her fair hills?"

Corum raised his head and got to his feet. Hanafax was already staring at the apparition on the rock above them.

"Who weeps, there?"

The woman was old. Her face was handsome and grim and white and lined. Her grey hair swirled about her and she was dressed in a red cloak such as the warriors had worn, mounted on a similar horned beast. She was a Vadhagh woman and very frail. Where her eyes had been were white, filmy pools of pain.

"I am Corum Jhaelen Irsei, lady. Why are you blind?"

"I am blind through choice. Rather than witness what had become of my land, I plucked my eyes from my head. I am Ooresé, Queen of Cira-an-Venl, and my people number twenty."

Corum's lips were dry. "I have slain your people, lady. That is why I weep."

Her face did not alter. "They were doomed," she said, "to die. It is better that they are dead. I thank you, stranger, for releasing them. Perhaps you would care to release me also. I only live so that the memory of Cira-an-Venl may live." She paused. "Why do you use a Vedragh name?"

"I am of the Vadhagh—the Vedragh, as you call them—I am from the lands far to the south."

"So Vedragh did go south. And is their land sweet?"

"It is very sweet."

"And are your folk happy, Prince Corum in the Scarlet Robe?"

"They are dead, Queen Ooresé. They are dead."

"All dead, then, now? Save you?"

"And save yourself, my queen."

A smile touched her lips. "He said we should all die, wherever we were, on whichever plane we existed. But there was another prophecy—that when we died, so did he. He chose to ignore it, as I remember."

"Who said that, lady?"

"The Knight of the Swords. Duke Arioch of Chaos. He who inherited these five planes for his part in that long-ago battle between Order and Chaos. Who came here and willed that smooth rock cover our pretty hills, that boiling lava run in our gentle streams, that flame spring where green forests had been. Duke Arioch, prince, made that prediction. But, before he departed to the place of his banishment, Lord Arkyn made another."

"Lord Arkyn?"

"Lord of Law, who ruled here before Arioch ousted him. He said that by destroying the Old Races, he would destroy his own power over the Five Planes."

"A pleasant wish," murmured Hanafax, "but I doubt if that is true."

"Perhaps we do deceive ourselves with happy lies, you who speak with the accent of a Mabden. But then you do not know what we know, for you are Arioch's children."

Hanafax drew himself up. "His children we may be, Queen

Ooresé, but his slaves we are not. I am here because I defied Arioch's will."

Again she smiled her sad smile. "And some say that the Vedragh doom was of their own doing. That they fought the Nhedregh and so defied Lord Arkyn's scheme of things."

"The gods are vengeful," Hanafax murmured.

"But I am vengeful, too, Sir Mabden," the queen said.

"Because we killed your warriors?"

She waved an ancient hand in a gesture of dismissal. "No. They attacked you. You defended yourselves. That is what that is. I speak of Duke Arioch and his whim—the whim that turned a beautiful land into this dreadful wasteland of eternal flame."

"You would be revenged, then, on Duke Arioch?" Corum said.

"My people once numbered hundreds. One after the other I sent them through the Lion's Mouth to destroy the Knight of the Swords. None did so. None returned."

"What is the Lion's Mouth?" Hanafax asked. "We heard it was the only escape from the Flamelands."

"It is. And it is no escape. Those who survive the passage through the Lion's Mouth do not survive what lies beyond it— the palace of Duke Arioch himself."

"Can none survive?"

The Blind Queen's face turned towards the rosy sky. "Only a great hero, Prince in the Scarlet Robe. Only a great hero."

"Once the Vadhagh had no belief in heroes and such," Corum said bitterly.

She nodded. "I remember. But then they needed no beliefs of that kind."

Corum was silent for a moment. Then he said, "Where is the Lion's Mouth, queen?"

"I will lead you to it, Prince Corum."

THROUGH THE LION'S MOUTH

THE QUEEN GAVE them water from the cask that rested behind her saddle and called up two of the lumbering mounts for Corum and Hanafax to ride. They climbed onto the beasts, clasped the reins, and then began to follow her over the black-and-green obsidian slabs, between the rivers of flame.

Though blind, she guided her beast skillfully, and she talked all the while of what had been here, what had grown there, as if she remembered every tree and flower that had once bloomed in her ruined land.

After a good space of time she stopped and pointed directly ahead. "What do you see there?"

Corum peered through the rippling smoke. "It looks like a great rock..."

"We will ride closer," she said.

And as they rode closer, Corum began to see what it was. It was, indeed, a gigantic rock. A rock of smooth and shining stone that glowed like mellowed gold. And it was fashioned, in perfect detail, to resemble the head of a huge lion with its sharp-fanged mouth wide open in a roar.

"Gods! Who made such a thing?" Hanafax murmured.

"Arioch created it," said Queen Ooresé. "Once our peaceful city lay there. Now we live—lived—in caves below the ground where water runs and it is a little cooler."

Corum stared at the enormous lion's head and he looked at Queen Ooresé. "How old are you, queen?"

"I do not know. Time does not exist in the Flamelands. Perhaps ten thousand years."

Far away another wall of flame danced. Corum remarked upon it.

"We are surrounded by flame on all sides. When Arioch first created it, many flung themselves into it rather than look upon what had become of their land. My husband died in that manner and thus did my brothers and all my sisters perish."

Corum noticed that Hanafax was not his usual talkative self. His head was bowed and he rubbed at it from time to time as if puzzled.

"What is it, friend Hanafax?"

"Nothing, Prince Corum. A pain in my head. Doubtless the heat causes it."

Now a singular moaning sound came to their ears. Hanafax looked up, his eyes wide and uncomprehending. "What is it?"

"The Lion sings," said the queen. "He knows we approach."

Then from Hanafax's throat a similar sound issued, as a dog will imitate another's howling.

"Hanafax, my friend!" Corum rode his beast close to the

other's. "Is something ailing you?"

Hanafax stared at him vaguely. "No. I told you, the heat…" His face twisted. "Aah! The pain! I will not! I will not!"

Corum turned to Queen Ooresé. "Have you known this happen before?"

She frowned, seeming to be thinking rather than displaying concern for Hanafax. "No," she said at last. "Unless…"

"*Arioch! I will not!*" Hanafax began to pant.

Then Corum's borrowed hand leapt up from the saddle where it had held the reins.

Corum tried to control it, but it shot straight towards Hanafax's face, its fingers extended. Fingers drove into the Mabden's eyes. They pierced the head, plunging deep into the brain. Hanafax screamed. "No, Corum, please do not… I can fight it… *aaaah!*"

And the Hand of Kwll withdrew itself, the fingers dripping with Hanafax's blood and brains, while the lifeless body of the Mabden fell from the saddle.

"What is happening?" Queen Ooresé called.

Corum stared at the mired hand, now once again his. "It is nothing," he murmured. "I have killed my friend."

He looked up suddenly.

Above him, on a hill, he thought he saw the outline of a figure watching him. Then smoke drifted across the scene and he saw nothing.

"So you guessed what I guessed, Prince in the Scarlet Robe," said the queen.

"I guessed nothing. I have killed my friend, that is all I know. He helped me. He showed me…" Corum swallowed with difficulty.

"He was only a Mabden, Prince Corum. Only a Mabden servant of Arioch."

"He hated Arioch!"

"But Arioch found him and entered him. He would have tried to kill us. You did right to destroy him. He would have betrayed you, prince."

Corum stared at her through brooding eyes. "I should have let him kill me. Why should I live?"

"Because you are of the Vedragh. The last of the Vedragh who can avenge our race."

"Let it perish, unrevenged! Too many crimes have been committed so that that vengeance might be won! Too many unfortunates have suffered frightful fates! Will the Vadhagh name be recalled with love—or muttered in hatred?"

"It is already spoken with hatred. Arioch has seen to that. There is the Lion's Mouth. Farewell, Prince in the Scarlet Robe!" And Queen Oorésé spurred her beast into a gallop and went plunging past the great rock, on towards the vast wall of flame beyond.

Corum knew what she would do.

He looked at the body of Hanafax. The cheerful fellow would smile no more and his soul was now doubtless suffering at the whim of Arioch.

Again, he was alone.

He gave a shuddering sigh.

The strange, moaning sound once again began to issue from the Lion's Mouth. It seemed to be calling him. He shrugged. What did it matter if he perished? It would only mean that no more would die because of him.

Slowly, he began to ride towards the Lion's Mouth. As he drew nearer, he gathered speed and then, with a yell, plunged through the gaping jaws and into the howling darkness beyond!

* * *

The beast stumbled, lost its footing, fell. Corum was thrown clear, got up, sought the reins with his groping hands. But the beast had turned and was galloping back towards the daylight that flickered red and yellow at the entrance.

For an instant Corum's mind cooled and he made to follow it. Then he remembered the dead face of Hanafax and he turned and began to trudge into the deeper darkness.

He walked thus for a long while. It was cool within the Lion's Mouth and he wondered if Queen Ooresé had been voicing nothing more than a superstition, for the interior seemed to be just a large cave.

Then the rustling sounds began.

He thought he glimpsed eyes watching. Accusing eyes? No. Merely malevolent. He drew his sword. He paused, looking about him. He took another step forward.

He was in whirling nothingness. Colours flashed past him, something shrieked and laughter filled his head. He tried to take another step.

He stood on a crystal plain and embedded in it, beneath his feet, were millions of beings—Vadhagh, Nhadragh, Mabden, Ragha-da-Kheta, and many others he did not recognize. There were males and females and all had their eyes open; all had their faces pressed against the crystal; all stretched out their hands as if seeking aid. All stared at him. He tried to hack at the crystal with his sword, but the crystal would not crack.

He moved forward.

He saw all the Five Planes, one superimposed upon the other, as he had seen them as a child—as his ancestors had known them. He was in a canyon, a forest, a valley, a field, another forest. He made to move into one particular plane, but he was stopped.

Screaming things came at him and pecked at his flesh. He fought them off with his sword. They vanished.

He was crossing a bridge of ice. It was melting. Fanged, distorted things waited for him below. The ice creaked. He lost his footing. He fell.

He fell into a whirlpool of seething matter that formed shapes and then destroyed them instantly. He saw whole cities brought into existence and then obliterated. He saw creatures, some beautiful, some disgustingly ugly. He saw things that made him love them and things that made him scream with hatred.

And he was back in the blackness of the great cavern where things tittered at him and scampered away from beneath his feet.

And Corum knew that anyone who had experienced the horrors that he had experienced would have been quite mad by now. He had gained something from Shool the sorcerer besides the Eye of Rhynn and the Hand of Kwll. He had gained an ability to face the most evil of apparitions and be virtually unmoved.

And, he thought, this meant that he had lost something, too…

He moved on another step.

He stood knee-deep in slithering flesh that was without shape but which lived. It began to suck him down. He struck about him with his sword. Now he was waist-deep. He gasped and forced his body through the stuff.

He stood beneath a dome of ice and with him stood a million Corums. There he was, innocent and gay before the coming of the Mabden, there he was moody and grim, with his jeweled eye and his murderous hand, there he was dying…

Another step.

Blood flooded over him. He tried to regain his feet. The heads of foul reptilian creatures rose from the stuff and snapped at his face with their jaws.

His instinct was to draw back. But he swam towards them.

He stood in a tunnel of silver and gold. There was a door at the end and he could hear movement behind it.

Sword in hand, he stepped through.

Strange, desperate laughter filled the immense gallery in which he found himself.

He knew that he had reached the Court of the Knight of the Swords.

THE GOD FEASTERS

CORUM WAS DWARFED by the hugeness of the hall. Suddenly he saw his past adventures, his emotions, his desires, his guilts as utterly inconsequential and feeble. This mood was increased by the fact that he had expected to confront Arioch the moment he reached his Court.

But Corum had entered the palace completely unnoticed. The laughter came from a gallery high above where two scaled demons with long horns and longer tails were fighting. As they fought, they laughed, though both seemed plainly near death.

It was on this fight that Arioch's attention seemed fixed.

The Knight of the Swords—the Duke of Chaos—lay in a heap of filth and quaffed some ill-smelling stuff from a dirty goblet. He was enormously fat and the flesh trembled on him as he laughed. He was completely naked and formed in all details like a Mabden. There seemed to be scabs and sores on his body, particularly near his pelvis. His face was flushed and it was ugly and his teeth, when he opened his mouth, seemed decayed.

Corum would not have known he was the god at all if it had not been for his size, for Arioch was as large as a castle and his sword, the symbol of his power, would have stood as high as the tallest tower of Castle Erorn, if it had been placed upright.

The sides of the hall were tiered. Uncountable tiers stretched high towards the distant dome of the ceiling which, itself, was wreathed in greasy smoke. These tiers were occupied, mainly with Mabden of all ages. Corum saw that most were naked. In many of the tiers they were copulating, fighting, torturing each other. Elsewhere were other beings—mainly scaly Shefanhow somewhat smaller than the two who were fighting together.

The sword was jet-black and carved with many peculiar patterns. Mabden were at work on the sword. They knelt on the blade and polished part of a design, or they climbed the hilt and washed it, or they sat astride the handgrip and mended the gold wire which bound it.

And other beings were busy, too. Like lice, they scampered and crawled over the god's huge bulk, picking at his skin, feeding off his blood and his flesh. Of all these activities, Arioch seemed oblivious. His interest continued to be the fight to the death in the gallery above.

Was this, then, the all-powerful Arioch, living like a drunken farmer in a pig sty? Was this the malevolent creature which had destroyed whole nations, which pursued a vendetta upon all the races to spring up on the Earth before his coming?

Arioch's laughter shook the floor. Some of the parasitic Mabden fell off his body. A few were unhurt, while others lay with their backs or their limbs broken, unable to move. Their comrades ignored their plight and patiently climbed again upon the god's body, tearing tiny pieces from him with their teeth.

Arioch's hair was long, lank and oily. Here, too, Mabden

searched for and fought over the bits of food that clung to the strands. Elsewhere in the god's body hair Mabden crept in and out, hunting for scraps and crumbs or tender portions of his flesh.

The two demons fell back. One of them was dead, the other almost dead but still laughing weakly. Then the laughter stopped.

Arioch slapped his body, killing a dozen or so Mabden, and scratched his stomach. He inspected the bloody remains in his palm and absently wiped them on his hair. Living Mabden seized the scraps and devoured them.

Then a huge sigh issued from the god's mouth and he began to pick his nose with a dirty finger that was the size of a tall poplar.

Corum saw that there were openings beneath the galleries and stairways twisting upwards, but he had no notion where the highest tower of the palace might be. He began to move, soft-footed, around the hall.

Arioch's ears caught the sound and the god became alert. He bent his head and peered about the floor. The huge eyes fixed on Corum and a monstrously large hand reached out to grasp him.

Corum raised his sword and hacked at the hand, but Arioch laughed and drew the Vadhagh prince towards him.

"What's this?" the voice boomed. "Not one of mine. Not one of mine."

Corum continued to strike at the hand and Arioch continued to seem unaware of the blows, though the sword raised deep cuts in the flesh. From over his shoulders, behind his ears and from within his filthy hair, Mabden eyes regarded Corum with terrified curiosity.

"Not one of mine," Arioch boomed again. "One of his. Aye. One of his."

"Whose?" Corum shouted, still struggling.

"The one whose castle I recently inherited. The dour fellow.

Arkyn. Arkyn of Law. One of his. I thought they were all gone by now. I cannot keep an eye on little beings not of my own manufacture. I do not understand their ways."

"Arioch! You have destroyed all my kin!"

"Ah, good. All of them, you say? Good. Is that the message you bring me? Why did I not hear before, from one of my own little creatures?"

"Let me go!" Corum screamed.

Arioch opened his hand and Corum staggered free, gasping. He had not expected Arioch to comply.

And then the full injustice of his fate struck him. Arioch bore no malice towards the Vadhagh. He cared for them no more or less than he cared for the Mabden parasites feeding off his body. He was merely wiping his palette clean of old colours as a painter will before he begins a fresh canvas. All the agony and the misery he and his had suffered was on behalf of the whim of a careless god who only occasionally turned his attention to the world that he had been given to rule.

Then Arioch vanished.

Another figure stood in his place. All the Mabden were gone.

The other figure was beautiful and looked upon Corum with a kind of haughty affection. He was dressed all in black and silver, with a miniature version of the black sword at his side. His expression was quizzical. He smiled. He was the quintessence of evil.

"Who are you?" Corum gasped.

"I am Duke Arioch, your master. I am the Lord of Hell, a Noble of the Realm of Chaos, the Knight of the Swords. I am your enemy."

"So you are my enemy. The other form was not your true form!"

"I am anything you please, Prince Corum. What does 'true' mean in this context? I can be anything I choose—or anything you choose, if you prefer. Consider me evil and I will don the appearance of evil. Consider me good—and I will take on a form that fits the part. I care not. My only wish is to exist in peace, you see. To while away my time. And if you wish to play a drama, some game of your own devising, I will play it until it begins to bore me."

"Were your ambitions ever thus?"

"What? What? Ever? No, I think not. Not when I was embattled with those Lords of Law who ruled this plane before. But now I have won, I deserve what I fought for. Do not all beings demand the same?"

Corum nodded. "I suppose they do."

"Well," Arioch smiled. "What now, little Corum of the Vadhagh? You must be destroyed soon, you know. For my peace of mind, you understand, that is all. You have done well to reach my Court. I will give you hospitality as a reward and then, at some stage, I will flick you away. You know why now."

Corum glowered. "I will *not* be 'flicked' away, Duke Arioch. Why should I be?"

Arioch raised a hand to his beautiful face and he yawned. "Why should you not be? Now. What can I do to entertain you?"

Corum hesitated. Then he said, "Will you show me all your castle? I have never seen anything so huge."

Arioch raised an eyebrow. "If that is all…?"

"All for the moment."

Arioch smiled. "Very well. Besides, I have not seen all of it myself. Come." He placed a soft hand on Corum's shoulder and led him through a doorway.

* * *

As they walked along a magnificent gallery with walls of coruscating marble, Arioch spoke reasonably to Corum in a low, hypnotic voice. "You see, friend Corum, these fifteen planes were stagnating. What did you Vadhagh and the rest do? Nothing. You hardly moved from your cities and your castles. Nature gave birth to poppies and daisies. The Lords of Law made sure that all was properly ordered. Nothing was happening at all. We have brought so much more to your world, my brother Mabelode and my sister Xiombarg."

"Who are the others?"

"You know them, I think, as the Queen of the Swords and the King of the Swords. They each rule five of the other ten planes. We won them from the Lords of Law a little while ago."

"And began your destruction of all that is truthful and wise."

"If you say so, mortal."

Corum paused. His understanding was weakening to Arioch's persuasive voice. He turned. "I think you are lying to me, Duke Arioch. There must be more to your ambition than this."

"It is a matter of perspective, Corum. We follow our whims. We are powerful now and nothing can harm us. Why should we be vindictive?"

"Then you will be destroyed as the Vadhagh were destroyed. For the same reasons."

Arioch shrugged. "Perhaps."

"You have a powerful enemy in Shool of Svi-an-Fanla-Brool! You should fear him, I think."

"You know of Shool, then?" Arioch laughed musically. "Poor Shool. He schemes and plots and maligns us. He is amusing, is he not?"

"He is merely amusing?" Corum was disbelieving.

"Aye—merely amusing."

"He says you hate him because he is almost as powerful as yourself."

"We hate no-one."

"I mistrust you, Arioch."

"What mortal does not mistrust a god?"

Now they were walking up a spiral ramp that seemed comprised entirely of light.

Arioch paused. "I think we will explore some other part of the palace. This leads only to a tower." Ahead Corum saw a doorway on which pulsed a sign—eight arrows arranged around a circle.

"What is that sign, Arioch?"

"Nothing at all. The Arms of Chaos."

"Then what lies beyond the door?"

"Just a tower." Arioch became impatient. "Come. There are more interesting sights elsewhere."

Reluctantly, Corum followed him back down the ramp. He thought he had seen the place where Arioch kept his heart.

For several more hours they wandered through the palace, observing its wonders. Here all was light and beauty and there were no sinister sights. This fact disturbed Corum. He was sure that Arioch was deceiving him.

They returned to the hall.

The Mabden lice had vanished. The filth had disappeared. In its place was a table laden with food and wine. Arioch gestured towards it.

"Will you dine with me, Prince Corum?"

Corum's grin was sardonic. "Before you destroy me?"

Arioch laughed. "If you wish to continue your existence a while longer, I have no objection. You cannot leave my palace, you see. And while your naïveté continues to entertain me, why should I destroy you?"

"Do you not fear me at all?"

"I fear you not at all."

"Do you not fear what I represent?"

"What do you represent?"

"Justice."

Again Arioch laughed. "Oh, you think so narrowly. There is no such thing!"

"It existed when the Lords of Law ruled here."

"Everything may exist for a short while—even justice. But the true state of the universe is anarchy. It is the mortal's tragedy that he can never accept this."

Corum could not reply. He seated himself at the table and began to eat. Arioch did not eat with him, but sat on the other side of the table and poured himself some wine. Corum stopped eating. Arioch smiled.

"Do not fear, Corum. It is not poisoned. Why should I resort to such things as poison?"

Corum resumed eating. When he had finished he said, "Now I would rest, if I am to be your guest."

"Ah." Arioch seemed perplexed. "Yes—well, sleep, then." He waved his hand and Corum fell face forward upon the table.

And slept.

THE BANE OF THE SWORD RULERS

CORUM STIRRED AND forced his eyes open. The table had gone. Gone, too, was Arioch. The vast hall was in darkness, illuminated only by faint light issuing from a few of the doorways and galleries.

He stood up. Was he dreaming? Or had he dreamed everything that had happened earlier? Certainly all the events had had the quality of dreams become reality. But that was true of the entire world now, since he had left the sanity of Castle Erorn so long ago.

But where had Duke Arioch gone? Had he left on some mission of the world? Doubtless he had thought his influence over Corum would last longer. After all, that was why he wished the Vadhagh all destroyed, because he could not understand them, could not predict everything they would do, could not control their minds as he controlled those of the Mabden.

Corum realized suddenly that he now had an opportunity, perhaps his only opportunity, to try to reach the place where Arioch kept his heart. Then he might escape while Arioch was still away, get back to Shool and reclaim Rhalina. Vengeance now no longer motivated him. All he sought was an end to his adventure, peace with the woman he loved, security in the old castle by the sea.

He ran across the floor of the hall and up the stairway to the gallery with the walls of coruscating marble until he came to the ramp that seemed made of nothing but light. The light had dimmed to a glow now, but high above was the doorway with the pulsating orange sign—the eight arrows radiating from a central hub—the Sign of Chaos.

Breathing heavily, he ran up the spiral ramp. Up and up he ran, until the rest of the palace lay far below him, until he reached the door which dwarfed him, until he stopped and looked and wondered, until he knew he'd reached his goal.

The huge sign pulsed regularly, like a living heart itself, and it bathed Corum's face and body and armour in its red-gold light. Corum pushed at the door, but it was like a mouse pushing at the door of a sarcophagus. He could not move it.

He needed aid. He contemplated his left hand—the Hand of Kwll. Could he summon help from the dark world? Not without a 'prize' to offer them.

But then the Hand of Kwll bunched itself into a fist and began to glow with a light that blinded Corum and made him stretch his arm away as far as it would go, flinging his other arm over his eyes. He felt the Hand of Kwll rise into the air and then strike at the mighty door. He heard a sound like the tolling of bells. He heard a crack as if the Earth herself had split. And then the Hand of Kwll was limp by his side and he opened his eyes and saw that a crack had appeared in the door. It was a small crack in the bottom of the right corner, but it was large enough for Corum to wriggle through.

"Now you are aiding me as I would wish to be aided," he

murmured to the hand. He got down on his knees and crawled through the crack.

Another ramp stretched upwards over a gulf of sparkling emptiness. Strange sounds filled the air, rising and dying, coming close and then falling away. There were hints of menace here, hints of beauty, hints of death, hints of everlasting life, hints of terror, hints of tranquility. Corum made to draw his sword and then realized the uselessness of such an action. He set foot on the ramp and began to climb again.

A wind seemed to spring up and his scarlet robe flew out behind him. Cool breezes wafted him and hot winds scoured his skin. He saw faces all around him and many of the faces he thought he recognized. Some of the faces were huge and some were infinitely tiny. Eyes watched him. Lips grinned. A sorrowful moaning came and went. A dark cloud engulfed him. A tinkling as of glass bells ringing filled his ears. A voice called his name and it echoed and echoed and echoed away for ever. A rainbow surrounded him, entered him and made his whole body flash with colour. Steadily he continued his walk up the long ramp.

And now he saw he was coming to a platform that was at the end of the ramp but which hung over the gulf. There was nothing beyond it.

On the platform was a dais. On the dais was a plinth and on the plinth was something that throbbed and gave forth rays.

Transfixed by these rays were several Mabden warriors. Their bodies were frozen in attitudes of reaching for the source of the rays, but their eyes moved as they saw Corum approach the dais. Pain was in those eyes, and curiosity, and a warning.

Corum stopped.

The thing on the plinth was a deep, soft blue and it was quite small and it shone and it looked like a jewel that had been fashioned into the shape of a heart. At every pulse, tubes of light shot forth from it.

This could only be the Heart of Arioch.

But it protected itself, as was evident from the frozen warriors surrounding it.

Corum took a pace nearer. A beam of light struck his cheek and it tingled.

Another pace nearer and two more beams of light hit his body and made it shiver, but he was not frozen. And now he was past the Mabden warriors. Two more paces and the beams bombarded his whole head and body, but the sensation was only pleasant. He stretched out his right hand to seize the heart, but his left hand moved first and the Hand of Kwll gripped the Heart of Arioch.

"The world seems full of fragments of gods," Corum murmured. He turned and saw that the Mabden warriors were no longer frozen. They were rubbing at their faces, sheathing their swords.

Corum spoke to the nearest. "Why did you seek the Heart of Arioch?"

"Through no choice of my own. A sorcerer sent me, offering me my life in return for stealing the heart from Arioch's palace."

"Was this Shool?"

"Aye—Shool. Prince Shool."

Corum looked at the others. They were all nodding. "Shool sent me!"

"And me!"

"And Shool sent me," said Corum. "I had not realized he had tried so many times before."

"It is a game Arioch plays with him," murmured one of the Mabden warriors. "I learned that Shool has little power of his own at all. Arioch gives Shool the power he thinks is his own, for Arioch enjoys the sport of having an enemy with whom he can play. Every action Arioch makes is inspired by nothing but boredom. And now you have his heart. Plainly he did not expect the game to get so out of hand."

"Aye," Corum agreed. "It was only Arioch's carelessness that allowed me to reach this place. Now, I return. I must find a way from the palace before he realizes what has happened."

"May we come with you?" the Mabden asked.

Corum nodded. "But hurry."

They crept back down the ramp.

Halfway down, one of the Mabden screamed, flailed at the air, staggered to the edge of the ramp and went drifting down into the sparkling emptiness.

Their pace increased until they reached the tiny crack at the bottom of the huge door and crawled through it, one by one.

Down the ramp of light they went. Through the gallery of coruscating marble. Down the stairway into the darkened hall.

Corum sought the silver door through which he had entered the palace. He made one complete circuit of the hall and his feet were aching before he realized that the door had vanished.

The hall was suddenly alive with light again and the vast, fat figure Corum had originally seen was laughing on the floor, lying amidst filth, with the Mabden parasites peering from out of the hair beneath his arms, from his navel, from his ears.

"Ha, ha! You see, Corum, I am kind! I have let you have almost everything you desired of me. You even have my heart! But I cannot let you take it away from me, Corum. Without my heart, I could not rule here. I think I will restore it into this flesh of mine."

Corum's shoulders slumped. "He has tricked us," he said to

his terrified Mabden companions.

But one Mabden said, "He has used you, Sir Vadhagh. He could never have taken his heart himself. Did you not know that?"

Arioch laughed and his belly shook and Mabden fell to the floor. "True! True! You have done me a service, Prince Corum. The heart of each Sword Ruler is kept in a place that is banned to him, so that the others may know that he dwells only in his own domain and may travel to no other, thus he cannot usurp some rival ruler's power. But you, Corum, with your ancient blood, with your peculiar characteristics, were able to do that which I am unable to do. Now I have my heart and I may extend my domain wherever I choose. Or not, of course, if I choose not to."

"Then I have helped you," Corum said bitterly, "when I wished to hinder you…"

Arioch's laughter filled the hall. "Yes. Exactly. A fine joke, eh? Now, give me my heart, little Vadhagh."

Corum pressed his back to the wall and drew his blade. He stood there with the Heart of Arioch in his left hand and his sword in his right. "I think I will die first, Arioch."

"As you please."

The monstrous hand reached out for Corum. He dodged it. Arioch bellowed with laughter again and plucked two of the Mabden warriors from the floor. They screamed and writhed as he drew them towards his great, wet mouth, full of blackened teeth. Then he popped them into his maw and Corum heard their bones crunch. Arioch swallowed and spat out a sword. Then he returned his gaze to Corum.

Corum jumped behind a pillar. Arioch's hand came round it, feeling for him. Corum ran.

More laughter and the hall reverberated. The god's mirth was echoed by the tittering voices of his Mabden parasites. A pillar crashed as Arioch struck at it, seeking Corum.

Corum dashed across the floor of the hall, leaping over the broken bodies of the Mabden who had fallen from the corpulent body of the god.

And then Arioch saw him, seized him, and his chuckles subsided.

"Give me my heart now."

Corum gasped for breath and freed his two hands from the soft flesh that enclosed him. The giant's great hand was warm and filthy. The nails were broken.

"Give me my heart, little being."

"No!" Corum drove his sword deep into the thumb, but the god did not notice. Mabden clung to the hair of the chest and watched, their grins blank.

Corum's ribs were near to breaking, but still he would not release the Heart of Arioch that lay in his left fist.

"No matter," said Arioch, his grip relaxing a trifle, "I can absorb both you and the heart at the same time."

Now Arioch began to carry his great hand towards his open mouth. His breath came out in stinking blasts and Corum choked on it, but still he stabbed and stabbed. A grin spread over the gigantic lips. All Corum could see now was that mouth, the scabrous nostrils, the huge eyes. The mouth opened wider to swallow him. He struck at the upper lip, staring into the red darkness of the god's throat.

Then his left hand contracted. It squeezed the Heart of Arioch. Corum's own strength could not have done it, but once again the Hand of Kwll was possessed of a power of its own. It squeezed.

Arioch's laughter faded. The vast eyes widened and a new light filled them. A bellow came from the throat.

The Hand of Kwll squeezed tighter still.

Arioch shrieked.

The heart began to crumble in the hand. Rays of a reddish blue light sprang from between Corum's fingers. Pain flooded up his arm.

There was a high whistling sound.

Arioch began to weep. His grasp on Corum weakened. He staggered backwards.

"No, mortal. No…" The voice was pathetic. "Please, mortal, we can…"

Corum saw the god's bloated form begin to melt into the air. The hand that held him began to lose its shape.

And then Corum was falling towards the floor of the hall, the broken pieces of Arioch's heart scattering as he fell. He landed with a crash, tried to rise, saw what was left of Arioch's body writhing in the air, heard a mournful sound, and then Corum lost consciousness, hearing, as he did so, Arioch's last whispered words.

"Corum of the Vadhagh. You have won the eternal bane of the Sword Rulers…"

A PAUSE IN THE STRUGGLE

ORUM SAW A *procession passing him.*

Beings of a hundred different races marched or rode or were carried in that procession and he knew that he watched all the mortal races that had ever existed since Law and Chaos had begun their struggle for domination over the multitudinous planes of the Earth.

In the distance, he saw the banners of Law and Chaos raised, side by side, the one bearing the eight radiating arrows, the other bearing the single straight arrow of Law. And over all this hung a huge balance in perfect equilibrium. In each of the balance's cups were marshaled other beings, not mortal. Corum saw Arioch and the Lords of Chaos in one and he saw the Lords of Law in the other.

And Corum heard a voice which said, "This is as it should be. Neither Law nor Chaos must dominate the destinies of the mortal planes. There must be equilibrium."

Corum cried out, "But there is no equilibrium. Chaos rules All!"

The voice replied, saying, "The Balance sometimes tips. It must be righted. And that is the power of mortals, to adjust the Balance."

"How may I do that?"

"You have begun the work already. Now you must continue until it is finished. You may perish before it is complete, but some other will follow you."

Corum shouted, "I do not want this. I cannot bear such a burden!"

"YOU MUST!"

The procession marched on, not seeing Corum, not seeing the two banners flying, not seeing the Cosmic Balance that hung over them.

Corum hung in cloudy space and his heart was at peace. Shapes began to appear and then he saw that he was back in Arioch's hall. He sought for his sword, but it was gone.

"I will return your sword before you leave, Prince Corum of the Vadhagh."

The voice was level and it was clear.

Corum turned.

He drew a sudden breath. "The Giant of Laahr!"

The sad, wise face smiled down on him. "I was called that, when I was in exile. But now I am no longer exiled and you may address me by my true name. I am Lord Arkyn and this is my palace. Arioch has gone. Without his heart he cannot assume flesh on these planes. Without flesh, he cannot wield power. I rule here now, as I ruled before."

The being's substance was still shadowy, though not as formless as before.

Lord Arkyn smiled. "It will take time before I assume my old form. Only by a great power of will did I enable myself to remain on this plane at all. I did not know when I rescued you, Corum, that you would be the cause of my restoration. I thank you."

"I thank you, my lord."

"Good breeds good," Lord Arkyn said. "Evil breeds evil."

Corum smiled. "Sometimes, my lord."

Lord Arkyn chuckled quietly. "Aye, you are right—sometimes. Well, mortal, I must return you to your own plane."

"Can you transport me to a particular place, my lord?"

"I can, Prince in the Scarlet Robe."

"Lord Arkyn, you know why I embarked upon this course of mine. I sought the remnants of the Vadhagh race, my folk. Tell me, are they all gone now?"

Lord Arkyn lowered his head. "All, save you."

"And cannot you restore them?"

"The Vadhagh were always the mortals I loved most, Prince Corum. But I have not the power to reverse the very cycle of time. You are the last of the Vadhagh. And yet..." Lord Arkyn paused. "And yet there might come a moment when the Vadhagh will return. But I see nothing clearly and I must speak no more of that."

Corum sighed. "Well, I must be content. And what of Shool? Is Rhalina safe?"

"I think so. My senses are still not capable of seeing all that happens and Shool was a thing of Chaos and is therefore much harder for me to see. But I believe that Rhalina is in danger, though Shool's power has waned with the passing of Arioch."

"Then send me, I beg you, to Svi-an-Fanla-Brool, for I love the Margravine."

"It is your capacity for love that makes you strong, Prince Corum."

"And my capacity for hate?"

"That directs your strength."

Lord Arkyn frowned, as if there was something he could not understand.

"You are sad in your triumph, Lord Arkyn? Are you always sad?"

The Lord of Law looked at Corum, almost in surprise. "I suppose I am still sad, yes. I mourn for the Vadhagh as you mourn. I mourn for the one who was killed by your enemy, Glandyth-a-Krae—the one you called the Brown Man."

"He was a good creature. Does Glandyth still bring death across the land of Bro-an-Vadhagh?"

"He does. You will meet him again, I think."

"And then I will kill him."

"Possibly."

Lord Arkyn vanished. The palace vanished.

Sword in hand, Corum stood before the low, twisted door that was the entrance to Shool's dwelling. Behind him, in the garden, the plants craned up to drink the rain that fell from a pale sky.

A peculiar calm hung over the dark and oddly formed building, but without hesitation Corum plunged into it and began to run down eccentric corridors.

"Rhalina! Rhalina!" The house muffled his shouts no matter how loudly he uttered them.

"Rhalina!"

Through the murky dwelling he ran until he heard a whining voice he recognized. Shool!

"Shool! Where are you?"

"Prince Shool. I will be given my proper rank. You mock me now my enemies have beaten me."

Corum entered a room and there was Shool. Corum recognized only the eyes. The rest was a withered, decrepit thing that lay upon a bed, unable to move.

Shool whimpered. "You, too, come to torment me now that I am conquered. Thus it always is with mighty men brought low."

"You only rose because it suited Arioch's sense of humour to let you."

"Silence! I will not be deceived. Arioch has taken vengeance upon me because I was more powerful than he."

"You borrowed, without knowing it, a fraction of his power. Arioch is gone from the Five Planes, Shool. You set events in motion which resulted in his banishment. You wanted his heart so that you might make him your slave. You sent many Mabden to steal it. All failed. You should not have sent me, Shool, for I did not fail and it resulted in your undoing."

Shool sobbed and shook his haggard head.

"Where is Rhalina, Shool? If she is harmed…"

"Harmed?" A hollow laugh from the wizened lips. "I harm her? It is she who placed me here. Take her away from me. I know she means to poison me."

"Where is she?"

"I gave you gifts. That new hand, that new eye. You would be crippled still if I had not been kind to you. But you will not remember my generosity, I know. You will—"

"Your 'gifts', Shool, near crippled my soul! Where is Rhalina?"

"Promise you will not hurt me, if I tell you?"

"Why should I wish to hurt so pathetic a thing as you, Shool? Now, tell me."

"At the end of the passage is a stair. At the top of the stair is a room. She has locked herself in. I would have made her my wife, you know. It would have been magnificent to be the wife of a god. An immortal. But she…"

"So you planned to betray me?"

"A god may do as he chooses."

Corum left the room, ran down the passage and up the short flight of stairs, hammering with the hilt of his sword upon the door.

"Rhalina!"

A weary voice came from beyond the door. "So your power has returned, Shool. You will not trick me again by disguising yourself as Corum. Though he be dead, I shall give myself to no other, least of all…"

"Rhalina! This really is Corum. Shool can do nothing. The Knight of the Swords has been banished from this plane and with him went Shool's sorcery."

"Is it true?"

"Open the door, Rhalina."

Cautiously bolts were drawn back and there was Rhalina. She was tired, she had plainly suffered much, but she was still beautiful. She looked deeply into Corum's face and her face flushed with relief, with love. She fainted.

Corum picked her up and began to carry her down the stairway, along the passage. He paused at Shool's room.

The one-time sorcerer was gone.

Suspecting a trick, Corum hurried to the main door.

Through the rain, along a path between the swaying plants, hurried Shool, his ancient legs barely able to carry him.

He darted a look back at Corum and chittered with fear. He dived into the bushes.

There was a smacking sound. A hiss. A wail.

Bile rose in Corum's throat. Shool's plants were feeding for the last time.

Warily he carried Rhalina along the path, tugging himself free from the vines and blooms that sought to hold him and kiss him, and at last he reached the shore.

A boat was tied up there, a small skiff which, with careful handling, would bear them back to Moidel's Castle.

The sea was smooth beneath the grey rain that fell upon it. On the horizon, the sky began to lighten.

Corum placed Rhalina gently in the boat and set sail for Moidel's Mount.

She woke up several hours later, looked at him, smiled sweetly, then fell asleep again.

Towards nightfall, as the boat sailed steadily homeward, she came and sat beside him. He wrapped his scarlet robe around her and said nothing.

As the moon rose, she reached up and kissed him on the cheek.

"I had not hoped…" she began. And then she wept for a little while and he comforted her.

"Corum," she said at length, "how has our luck improved so?"

And he began to tell her of what had befallen him. He told her of the Ragha-da-Kheta, of the magical kite, of the Flamelands, of Arioch and of Arkyn.

He told her all, save two things.

He did not tell her how he—or the Hand of Kwll—had murdered King Temgol-Lep, who had tried to poison him, or her countryman Hanafax, who had tried to help him.

When he had finished her brow was unclouded and she sighed with her happiness.

"So we have peace, at last. The conflict is over."

"Peace, if we are lucky, for a little while." The sun had begun to rise. He adjusted his course.

"You will not leave me again? Law rules now, surely, and…"

"Law rules only upon this plane. The Lords of Chaos will not be pleased with what has happened here. Arioch's last words to me were that I have incurred the bane of the Sword Rulers. And Lord Arkyn knows that much more must be done before Law is once again secure in the Fifteen Planes. And Glandyth-a-Krae will be heard of again."

"You will seek vengeance against him?"

"No longer. He was merely an instrument of Arioch. But he will not forget his hatred of me, Rhalina."

The sky cleared and was blue and golden. A warm breeze blew.

"Are we then, Corum, to have no peace?"

"We shall have some, I think. But it will be merely a pause in the struggle, Rhalina. Let us enjoy that pause while we may. We have won that much, at least."

"Aye." Her tone became merry. "And peace and love that are won are more greatly appreciated than if they are merely inherited!"

He held her in his arms.

The sun was strong in the sky. Its rays struck a jeweled hand and a jeweled eye and it made them burn brightly and flash like fire.

But Rhalina did not see them burning, for she slept again in Corum's arms.

Moidel's Mount came in sight. Its green slopes were washed by a gentle blue sea and the sun shone on its white stone castle. The tide was in, covering the causeway.

Corum looked down at Rhalina's sleeping face. He smiled and gently stroked her hair.

He saw the forest on the mainland. Nothing threatened.

He glanced up at the cloudless sky.

He hoped the pause would be a long one.

THIS ENDS THE FIRST BOOK OF CORUM

 ABOUT THE AUTHOR

Born in London in 1939, Michael Moorcock now lives in Texas. A prolific and award-winning writer with more than eighty works of fiction and non-fiction to his name, he is the creator of Elric, Jerry Cornelius and Colonel Pyat, amongst many other memorable characters. In 2008, *The Times* named Moorcock in their list of "The 50 greatest British writers since 1945".

**ALSO AVAILABLE FROM
TITAN BOOKS AND TITAN COMICS**

A NOMAD OF THE TIME STREAMS
The Warlord of the Air
The Land Leviathan
The Steel Tsar

THE ETERNAL CHAMPION SERIES
The Eternal Champion
Phoenix in Obsidian
The Dragon in the Sword

THE CORUM SERIES
The Queen of the Swords (June 2015)
The King of the Swords (July 2015)
The Bull and the Spear (August 2015)
The Oak and the Ram (September 2015)
The Sword and the Stallion (October 2015)

THE CORNELIUS QUARTET
The Final Programme (February 2016)
A Cure for Cancer (March 2016)
The English Assassin (April 2016)
The Condition of Muzak (May 2016)

THE MICHAEL MOORCOCK LIBRARY
Elric of Melniboné
Elric: Sailor on the Seas of Fate (June 2015)

MICHAEL MOORCOCK'S ELRIC
Volume 1: The Ruby Throne
Volume 2: Stormbringer